DUSK UNVEILED

A RAVENWOOD COVEN NOVEL

CARRIE ANN RYAN

DUSK UNVEILED

A Ravenwood Coven Novel

By Carrie Ann Ryan

Dusk Unveiled
A Ravenwood Coven Novel
By: Carrie Ann Ryan
© 2021 Carrie Ann Ryan
eBook ISBN: 978-1-950443-53-6
Paperback ISBN: 978-1-950443-54-3

Cover Art by Sweet N Spicy Designs

For Heather.
Thank you for all you do.

PRAISE FOR CARRIE ANN RYAN

"Count on Carrie Ann Ryan for emotional, sexy, character driven stories that capture your heart!" – Carly Phillips, NY Times bestselling author

"Carrie Ann Ryan's romances are my newest addiction! The emotion in her books captures me from the very beginning. The hope and healing hold me close until the end. These love stories will simply sweep you away." ~ NYT Bestselling Author Deveny Perry

"Carrie Ann Ryan writes the perfect balance of sweet and heat ensuring every story feeds the soul." - Audrey Carlan, #1 New York Times Bestselling Author

"Carrie Ann Ryan never fails to draw readers in with passion, raw sensuality, and characters that pop off the page. Any book by Carrie Ann is an absolute treat." – New York Times Bestselling Author J. Kenner

"Carrie Ann Ryan knows how to pull your heartstrings and make your pulse pound! Her wonderful Redwood Pack series will draw you in and keep you reading long into the night. I can't wait to see what comes next with the new generation, the Talons. Keep them coming, Carrie Ann!" –Lara Adrian, New York Times bestselling author of CRAVE THE NIGHT

"With snarky humor, sizzling love scenes, and brilliant, imaginative worldbuilding, The Dante's Circle series reads as if Carrie Ann Ryan peeked at my personal wish list!" – NYT Bestselling Author, Larissa Ione

"Carrie Ann Ryan writes sexy shifters in a world full of passionate happily-ever-afters." – *New York Times* Bestselling Author Vivian Arend

"Carrie Ann's books are sexy with characters you can't help but love from page one. They are heat and heart blended to perfection." *New York Times* Bestselling Author Jayne Rylon

Carrie Ann Ryan's books are wickedly funny and deliciously hot, with plenty of twists to keep you guessing. They'll keep you up all night!" USA Today Bestselling Author Cari Quinn

"Once again, Carrie Ann Ryan knocks the Dante's Circle series out of the park. The queen of hot, sexy, enthralling paranormal romance, Carrie Ann is an author not to miss!" *New York Times* bestselling Author Marie Harte

DUSK UNVEILED

NYT Bestselling Author Carrie Ann Ryan continues her magical paranormal series where a town keeps its secrets, but an aging curse might just be their downfall.

The Christopher curse is one of legend—so old that every new generation knows they will be touched by it. With every spell muttered, every magical pull needed to save her town, Laurel Christopher knows she's one step closer to burning to ash and leaving those she loves behind. She'll fight with all she has to protect her people—and the man she loves—but she might not have enough strength remaining to save herself.

Jaxton Dark lost his best friend to the necromancer attacking Ravenwood but refuses to lose his mate to a curse that could take them both. He's well aware of the loss calling them, but before he can stand up for those he loves, a betrayal cuts him to the core.

Sacrifice was always an inevitability when it comes to the curse that threatens their fate. Yet it's only when the darkness makes a subtle and surprising move that star-crossed lovers, Laurel and Jaxton, will truly find out the meaning of who they could be and what they must give up to survive.

CHAPTER
ONE

Laurel

The gravestone was more of a placard, really, one that shone under the fading sun and didn't mark a grave but more a remembrance.

Trace wasn't buried under my feet. His body wasn't here. His ashes had been spread to the wind. One of my best friends, the man I had thought would be my every-thing—or at least I had deluded myself into thinking would be my everything—was long gone. The only thing that remained was this placard his parents and the pack had wanted to use to remember him by and the memories that currently cascaded through my brain.

Trace was dead. Faith, a necromancer and dark witch, had killed him.

I still couldn't quite believe that I wouldn't hear his laughter again—that big belly laugh that warmed me from the inside out. He always made me smile, even if he made me growl more often than not. Since he was the bear shifter, he had constantly rolled his eyes and proceeded to show me exactly how I was supposed to growl instead of the weak little baby growl that escaped my human-witch lips.

I had loved Trace. Maybe not how others thought I should, not in the ways that would be forever and mean bonds and mates, but I *had* loved him.

He had been my friend first and foremost, and I'd thought maybe the fates would decide that we would be together, at least partially. Because I knew Trace wasn't my forever. He'd had the potential, but he hadn't truly been mine. And he wouldn't have been even if the world had allowed him to live. If Faith and the revenants hadn't taken him from me. From his family. His pack.

He had been my growly bear, my best friend, the one I could lean on when I thought the world might crash around me. He was the person I ran to when things got too complicated. When I had to hide from my family, my past, my curse, and...my hawk.

I frowned, wondering why I was so melancholic. No, that wasn't it. I knew. Because there was nothing good happening anymore.

"I miss you, Trace. I'd say it should have been me, but maybe it will be soon." I winced as I moved, the motion tugging on the new burn marks on my flesh. "It might be me soon if this curse has anything to say about it."

I rested on my knees in front of the placard, alone except for the forest's non-magical inhabitants. The bears of the Ravenwood den gave me time to speak to Trace. Some had assumed he would be my mate. Others just knew that we had been friends and wanted to give me peace.

I hated that I hadn't been strong or fast enough to save him.

As the curse currently working through my system reminded me repeatedly, I wasn't fast enough for many things. Because Trace had died, and I was following him.

Every time I used my magic to protect this town, myself, and my friends, the fire within me burned.

Every time I used my fire magic, the element that was closest to my soul, it killed me a little. I was one day closer to death, one step closer to the eternal torment that awaited me because of the curse on my family.

One that hadn't only affected me but also my sibling. Though my affliction was far different than my older brother, Ash's.

I was a fire witch, one of the Ravenwood coven. And I was broken.

Every time I used my fire, the flames licked up my body, scorching me from the inside out. I knew that one day, I would do one too many spells, and I would be gone. I would lose everything. And perhaps I deserved it.

I didn't know exactly what I had done, but I didn't have the strength that Rowen, my best friend and leader, had. I wasn't Sage, the new member, the water witch. The innocent who had come to our town so recently.

I loved them both; they were my sisters in everything but blood, but they would have to find a way to defeat the darkness without me. Perhaps Rowen would finally allow Ash to join the coven in truth, and he'd be the third to anchor the circle.

I knew I wasn't going to live much longer. The burns on my side and across my soul were evidence of that.

I needed to get back to town to work in the bookshop but I didn't want to leave Trace behind.

Only, he wasn't here. I had to remember that. He was gone. This plaque was only a place for those left behind to mourn and grieve. He wasn't here.

I stood, ignoring the painful stretch and tearing of my skin as I did. I straightened my shirt, making sure to cover the scars and burns. Nobody needed to realize the pain I was in or see how close I was to my end.

The only person I thought truly did was Jaxton—though I wasn't sure it was safe for him to know anymore.

Still, Jaxton always knew.

And that was why I pushed him away. Why I had clung to Trace when both of us knew we weren't each other's forever.

"You doing okay?" Ariel asked, and I turned, knowing the woman was there since my magic had alerted me to her presence, but I did my best not to flinch or show any signs of weakness. Ariel was the second in command, the beta of the Ravenwood bear pack. Rome, Sage's mate and a badass bear shifter, was the alpha. Ariel had been newly titled as beta.

Once Trace died, and Alden, the final triplet of the three bears also passed, Ariel stepped in.

I held back a growl, trying not to think about Alden. The traitor. The one who had wanted power so much, he'd gone to a necromancer for it. He had caused Trace's death. And the demise of so many others. I would never forgive him.

"From the look on your face, you're either thinking about Alden or Faith. Or this Oriel," Ariel said as she tilted her head, staring at me.

I held back a sigh. "A little bit of all of those. But mostly Alden."

Ariel's eyes glowed for a moment before she let out a breath, her bear at the surface. "I can't help but wonder if he would have changed if I had taken him out earlier. Forced him down the hierarchy in the pack. Maybe it would have been enough."

I shook my head, ignoring the tug on my skin as I moved towards the other woman. "No. You might have always been stronger than him and deserved to be third after Trace and Rome, but defeating Alden would have only pushed him closer to the edge sooner. Who knows what he might've done if given the chance?"

"I know you're right, but I still hate what he did to our pack. To Trace."

I nodded, pressing my lips together. "Same here. But we can't take it back. There's no going back."

"If only there were time witches."

I snorted. "I don't think that's how magic works. But who knows? Maybe you could ask Aspen."

Ariel beamed. "The leader of the fae *does* have some magnificent powers. Who knows? Maybe he *can* turn back time. He's seen many years of it, after all."

Aspen was the enigmatic fae leader in our tiny little town. There were fae, witches, humans, shifters, and other magical creatures living within the town's wards.

And everybody had secrets.

Ravenwood was special. It always had been.

I nodded in thanks and said goodbye to Ariel as I moved towards the town center, needing space. Ariel seemed to understand that. She must've been on patrol, protecting the lands around the den. I was grateful for it. The bears and other shifters guarded Ravenwood, just like the witches used their magic to clean up any messes, hide the existence of the paranormal from the rest of the world, and keep the wards surrounding the town limits stable and steady. We needed the magical boundaries to preserve the secrecy and to keep Oriel—and whoever else was in that darkness—out.

Only, we didn't seem to be strong enough, and I only had myself to blame. Sage was new, and she was only just now coming into her power after a curse had kept her away from us for so long. Now, she was mated to the bear alpha and learning her abilities to help Rowen keep the town safe.

I was the liability.

I nodded at Frank, an older jaguar who had come to Ravenwood years ago and hadn't left. He had once been faster than any other shifter within the town limits, but now he was a little older with arthritis in his hips. Still, he was so fast it was awe-inspiring to watch him move sometimes.

He tilted the brim of his hat towards me and then went into the small bakery that Sage owned and operated.

I smelled the yeast and bread in the air and groaned, my stomach growling. Sage was a fantastic baker and had brought beautiful things to our town. Before, we only had a little Italian place. It had some bread, but nothing like what Sage made and infused with her magic.

It was incredible. She was a great asset to the town.

I was just trying to be and do the same. I looked up at the bookstore sign and felt a slight twinge in my heart as I did. Sage's aunt, Penelope, had owned this bookshop. She had created it and had put her soul into it.

When the revenants and Faith killed her, it had left a gaping hole in the town and my soul. I had loved Penelope like my own family and had worked at the bookshop for as long as I could remember.

Yes, I still worked with my brother's business to help with real estate and other finances around the country and the globe, but now my primary source of work was the bookstore itself.

After Penelope's will had been read and the bookshop was split between Sage and me, I had cried. I had let others see my weakness and tears. I'd always thought of Penelope as family, and to know that she'd felt the same had staggered me. Sage had been the one to tell me that I should run it. She'd even tried to sign her half over to me, but I hadn't let her.

"She was your family. I should be the one letting you have it," I had said.

Sage had merely shaken her head. *"No, if you won't let me give you my half, then we'll both keep it. I'll run the bakery, you run the bookstore, and we can bring Penelope's memory and magic to this world."*

I had only nodded, touched beyond measure. Now, I did my best not to ruin the place that had brought me so much joy for so long.

The town was like any small town in Pennsylvania. Mom and Pop places lined Main Street, each with its own unique hand-carved wooden sign and colonial building that had likely been a home at one time. There were also minor roads with newer businesses that catered to more magical things than the books and pastries we offered on Main Street, where most of the businesses were located. Rowen's witchy antique shop was in a league of its own right on Main Street.

I loved the bookshop that brought me so much peace and joy, but I hated that part of me felt as if I would always miss Penelope. Because she wasn't here, and I was left to make sure her legacy didn't die.

My powers called to me, and I ignored them, knowing I couldn't even tempt fate with a minor spell. The bookshop needed me to be whole. A fire witch who couldn't control her powers without killing herself, surrounded by shifters, didn't always mix. I took a deep breath, but before I could step into the shop, I frowned and tilted my head as I listened.

There was a cry in the air, a hawk's screech, and I looked up to see Jaxton, the wing leader of the Ravenwood wing, and the man I couldn't let myself think about. He flew overhead, and I gripped the hilt of the sword behind me before moving forward and past the bookstore. I used a small spell to hide the sword from view, but because I couldn't use my powers and couldn't use spells that might kill me, I'd had to learn how to use the weapon.

And while within the town limits of Ravenwood, everyone knew of magic and the darkness and the powers that be, passersby weren't allowed to know. We used spells to conceal that, and Jaxton and Rome—as our fixers and cleaners—hid our existence from those who weren't part of the town.

Only it was a losing battle, and we all knew it.

However, I couldn't think about any of that. I had to remember the reason Jaxton had called us.

Sage and Rome ran out of the back of the building, the big bear ready to shift, his claws ripping through his fingertips, and his grizzly hump rising. I didn't know if he'd shift fully while still clothed, but he held power within him to partially shift—something not all shifters could do.

By his side, Sage's power filled her eyes and her entire being. She was turning into a powerful witch, and I wasn't jealous in the least. We needed her, especially when I was holding us back.

"I heard Jaxton call out to us as we set up the bakery. Do you know what's going on?" Sage asked.

I shook my head, pulling out my sword. I might not be able to set it aflame with a spell as easily as I had when I first lost my ability to use the magic I needed, but I could still fight with the blade better than anyone who lived within the town's wards. "I don't know, but that call means to come. So, here we are."

I ran toward the lake and pond areas behind Main Street, noticing out of the corner of my eye that Ash was coming, as well. My brother, the one who had left the town limits long ago and was only newly back, gave me a tight nod and moved. I felt his magic within him, but I didn't think he'd use it. Especially not when we could harm others. Ash used more than I did since his didn't hurt him—at least as far as I knew—but he mostly did spells rather than use the earth element he was connected to. His earth didn't crush him as my fire burned me.

Rowen followed us, her power immense, the air around her swirling. She didn't speak to us, didn't look our way. Though, I didn't even have to look behind me to know she was there.

She was *power*.

Despite the fact that her life force was currently being drained to within its last inch to protect the town.

Something was coming, and we needed to fight.

A scream rent the air near the lake behind Main Street, and I ran faster, only to see Nelle, our resident goth mermaid, pulling herself out of the water and pointing behind her. "Revenants. I think there's five." She screamed again as one pulled itself out of the water and scraped its nails down her finned flank. She shoved at him, but mermaids weren't as strong on land. They could walk on two legs, and they could move like a human, but they were their most powerful while in the water.

"Did you know revenants could swim?" Sage asked, and I shook my head, sword at the ready.

"Not in the slightest." I moved forward as the revenants came closer and slashed down at the closest one coming at Nelle.

"Damn it," she said as she shoved a dagger that had

been strapped to her arm into the revenant's skull. I pulled at the mermaid, gripping her arm as I got her out of the pond. She shook herself off, shifting into her human form. Her black scales turned into leather pants, and her chain and leather top remained the same since she didn't swim topless. She gave me a tight nod, her kohl-ringed eyes bright with magic. "I think he's the only one down there. The rest are up here."

I growled, reminding myself of Trace again. "Are you okay?"

She held her side and then showed me her bloody hand. "I'll be fine."

"Okay. Then, duck." She did as I said without question. I liked Nelle. I had known her since she was a baby, surprising all of us with her true form.

I slashed out with my sword, decapitating a revenant and wondering where the hell the necromancer was that controlled these undead bodies.

Nelle's eyes widened, and she tugged at me. I turned, frowning at her for trying to distract me. Suddenly, there was a shout and the sound of a hawk. I ducked, doing my best to cover Nelle's body as a fire stream soared overhead. My magic called out to me, singing its song of torment as it yearned to join with the magic and fight the only way it knew how.

Only I couldn't.

Not if I wanted to live.

"That wasn't me!" I called out, making sure every-body knew that I wasn't the one using the fire magic.

"There's another fire witch?" Nelle asked, and I tugged on her, trying to get us away from the flames.

And then Jaxton, hawk shifter, the man I couldn't allow to be my mate, a man who happened to be Nelle's half-brother, flew towards us, clawing out the eyes of a revenant who had been crawling our way. One I hadn't seen. I screamed as the second revenant's claws dug into my side, and I was afraid that Jaxton was too late.

Magic burned within me. It wanted out, but I needed to save Nelle. I needed to stop whatever was happening.

However, once again, it seemed that I might be too late.

Flames licked my side, and I watched the world burn.

Jaxton

Fire screamed around us before it died as quickly as it came, the furious tendrils threatening to sear our skin before it faded to nothingness. Laurel shouted that the magic wasn't from her, and since she wasn't scorched from the inside out, I had to believe her.

I looked down at both Laurel and Nelle and cursed under my breath before using my talons to rip off the head of the closest revenant. I held out my free hand. "Get up, Nelle. And stay behind me."

She pulled her dark hair away from her face and scowled, even as she kept her gaze on the battle in front of us. "If you would just let me have a sword like Laurel, I could fight."

"The sword is too heavy for you. We've been training with other weapons. Weapons you don't have on you since you just came out of the deep with the one dagger that's currently in the revenant's skull."

"Yes, so I can bash someone's head in but not slice it off. So helpful." She ducked out of the way as Laurel used her sword to impale the final revenant. My little sister glared at me.

"What?" I asked, my adrenaline pumping through my system. I hated the idea that Laurel was in pain, and that I'd almost lost my little sister. I hadn't even known that revenants could swim. But, apparently, they could. And now we would have to deal with yet another way for the monsters to attack our people. Go after my sister.

"Thanks for the assist," Laurel said as she slid her sword into her scabbard on her back and rolled her shoulders. She wore the blade on her back or on her hip, depending on the day. She was a master with the weapon and shifted where she carried it depending on the current scars on her body.

Neither Nelle nor I missed the wince on Laurel's face that she tried to cover up when she moved. She couldn't hide her pain from me. She had never been able to, which was probably why she constantly avoided me—or at least, part of the reason.

We hadn't spoken since the last time I was in her

home, and I had looked at her in the mirror, telling her it was time.

Of course, it was time. It was long past it. But Laurel wouldn't take that step. And I knew there was a reason for it. It would cost too much, and it could hurt so many, but I couldn't have Laurel die. I couldn't lose her when I'd only just now found her. Or rather, let myself believe I'd found her.

Only this wasn't about me. It would never be about me. It needed to be about Laurel, her choices, and the assholes trying to kill my sister and take over my goddamn town.

"Why are you glaring?" Nelle asked as she leaned forward, her voice a whisper.

"It's nothing."

"You should just tell her how you feel."

I glared down at Nelle, doing my best not to look too menacing. She was a sweet baby angel, at least according to our mother. A beautiful mermaid who could do no wrong.

My mom, like my father and me, was a hawk shifter. My father had died when I was a young boy, and my mother had found another mate, something not too unheard of but quite rare. Only that mate had been one of the merpeople who lived beneath the surface of the water. He rarely came up these days due to the uneasy wards and failing magic beneath the core of the town since Ravenwood couldn't hold itself to the paranormal world as it once had. As the alliance of witches faded through time and death, so did the magic tethering the town to the supernatural. My sister spent most of her time below the surface with her father these days, using their magic rather than ours.

My mother spent her days on land, trying to help me run the wing and baby my younger sister as much as possible. Because Nelle was half-hawk, half-mermaid—though only able to shift into her mer form—Nelle could go from the land to the water far easier than any of her full-blooded mer relatives.

That meant I saw my baby sister more than I would have in any other magical situation. And I hated to see her hurt. I looked down at the wound already healing on her side. "Are you okay?"

"I'm fine. It sliced through part of my fin, but not enough to keep me down. I didn't expect any revenants down there. Now we'll keep watch."

"Do you need to go down there now and explain to the others what happened?"

She shook her head, frowning. "No, Holden was already there." I scowled, and she rolled her eyes. "We both know that Holden's not for me, even if he wants his little mer princess."

My father had been the wing leader before I took over. And then he died far too young. So, my mother was left as the wing leader's mate—and influential in her own right. Of course, she ended up meeting with the king of the merpeople below the surface. Through magic beyond me, Nelle and the others could travel from water to water as long as the king was in charge of that particular area.

That meant when Nelle went below the surface, she wasn't only in the large pond or the lake in Ravenwood. She could also go to saltwater areas all over the world.

It was a quirk of the realms and magic that I had no part in and didn't understand. That also meant that Nelle was the princess of the merpeople and held power in her own right.

Even if she wasn't a full mermaid.

"I was going to go see Mom anyway. I'll follow when you go. I think she's coming below the surface later for an extended period, but I miss seeing her up here, especially in her hawk form. Are you going back to the wing? To tell them what happened?"

I heard my sister, but my gaze was on Laurel. She was studiously *not* looking at me, however.

I didn't blame her, but damn it, I wanted her to look at me. I needed her to see me. And she wasn't going to. If she did, she would realize what we were both ignoring. And see that she was afraid.

I wasn't. I *couldn't* be anymore.

I had given her enough time, enough slack. Now, I would do what I should've done a long time ago.

"You're growling. You're a hawk, not a bear. You don't growl."

I held back my smile, despite current circumstances. "I do what I have to."

"I need to go talk with the pack," Rome said, his arm around Sage's waist.

"I need to discuss what just happened with the wing." I nodded tightly.

"And we will have a coven meeting," Rowen added as she pulled her dark hair back from her face. I watched as Ash's gaze locked on her movements, but I didn't say anything. It seemed I wasn't the only one who wanted something I couldn't have.

"Is everyone okay?" I asked, my gaze moving around the others and the bodies at our feet.

"We are," Sage answered. "Are you okay, Nelle?"

My sister rubbed her side, her jewelry glittering in the sunlight. "I'm fine. I wanted to come and visit with you all topside and wasn't expecting the ambush. I honestly didn't realize revenants could go down that far."

"Or swim," Laurel ground out. I met her gaze and saw the pain and flames in her eyes. Did no one else see the burning? The agony that was slowly taking her from us all?

Did they all just think that she was fine and could make it through the spells? I had to wonder why she was hiding so much from them.

Because she was in pain. She was dying. With each spell, each magical moment, her body burned from the inside out.

I didn't know how they couldn't smell the burnt flesh or see the flames dancing in her eyes.

One day, she would become ash, and no one would be able to stop the magic from consuming her from within.

I didn't know what we would do then. What *I* would do.

We had already lost Trace.

Who would I become if I lost Laurel, too?

Do you need any healing? Any of you?" Rowen asked as she sidestepped ever so slightly away from Ash. I wasn't even sure she was aware she'd done it. But I saw it. We all did. The fact that she couldn't be near Ash even though part of her probably wanted to was obvious.

I didn't know how she did it. Then again, I kind of understood. I was living in my own new world.

"I'll have Mom take a look. But my fin, or rather my leg, is already healed."

"None of us got hit."

I looked at Laurel and narrowed my eyes. She rolled hers and held up her hands. "I'm fine. Mr. Hawk over there made sure of it."

"You could've been killed," I snapped.

"I wasn't. Thank you so much for taking care of me."

"You need to take better care of yourself!"

Why was I yelling at her? I couldn't fix things, so I kept lashing out.

She would probably hurt me later, and I would only have myself to blame.

"Stop fighting," Sage said as she rubbed her temples. "We had a break from this, a moment where we could all breathe. Now Oriel, or whoever he sent, is back. And we have to deal."

"You think it was just Oriel then? Or was it someone else?" Ash asked, his voice wooden.

I met his gaze then gestured over to my little sister. She knew some of what was going on, but not everything. The more she learned, the more likely it was that she'd get hurt beyond the scratches she received today.

I refused to let my baby sister be part of this.

"I saw that. You should let me help. Aspen and I want to help."

I froze and then glared at her. "Been speaking to Aspen a lot then, have you?" I asked, and Laurel snorted.

"Oh, you sweet baby angel, you're so adorable when you're clueless."

"Do you want to talk about clueless right now?" I asked, glaring.

"What did I just say about fighting?" Sage cut in.

Laurel snorted. "We're not fighting. We're talking. This is my voice."

"Petulant and confrontational?" Ash asked, and I snorted, enjoying that Ash could joke with us. He didn't often laugh. As if he had forgotten exactly who he was before the curse had taken place. And maybe parts of him had, but I didn't think that was all of it.

"Thanks for that," Laurel said as she punched her big

brother in the shoulder. "So glad to have you back in town and on my side."

"We all should be on the same side," Rowen stated as she pulled her hair back again. "And I broke my hair tie."

Laurel waved her hands in the air, though I saw the fear in her eyes. "Oh, no, whatever shall you do without your perfect little hair tie to keep your long, glorious locks away from your face?"

"Your hair looks as if you put your finger in an outlet and let it go into this glorious red fire. I wouldn't talk."

"Enough," Sage growled, the water in the pond behind her rising.

Nelle's eyes widened, and I tugged her away. "Come on. Let's get you to Mom and make sure you're going to heal." The skin had mended on its own thanks to her magic, but I never could be too careful when it came to my sister.

"So, we're just not going to talk about the fact that I mentioned Aspen?" she asked sweetly.

I let out a breath. I knew she was teasing to cut the tension, but I wasn't sure I could hold back my questions when it came to the fae king for long. "Let's go."

"We need to have a meeting. With the six of us," Sage replied, and Rowen narrowed her eyes. "The six of us. Not just those you get along with, Rowen."

I froze, wondering about Sage's tone. Sage never stood up to Laurel or Rowen. Mostly because she was still new to the group and figuring out our past truths and secrets.

Wading through the waters of our shared connections, even as they changed, wasn't easy.

The fact that Sage felt comfortable enough to stand up for herself now made me smile. She was learning her powers and her position in the town and within the coven.

Honestly, none of us had time to hold back. We needed to ensure that we were taking care of each other and finding out exactly who was trying to hurt our home.

"Coven meeting soon," Rowen said and nodded, her shoulders lowering. "All of us."

"Where we'll figure out if this was Oriel or someone else," I added.

"Let's hope it was just Oriel," Rowen said with a frown. "Because if it's someone else, then we have another necromancer out there, raising the dead from around the country and using their corpses for their own agenda."

Rome's bear rose to the surface as he spoke. "They won't take any more from us."

Laurel's chin lifted as she vowed, "I refuse it."

Ash and I remained silent.

"Same here. So, we figure it out. We'll meet and find out who did this. Now, let's make sure we're all healthy and take care of our town so we can." Sage nodded tightly and then spun on her heel and stomped back towards Main Street. Rome gave us all a look, lifted a shoulder, and followed her.

"Not that I don't like it, but when did Sage get all badass?" my little sister asked.

I shook my head. "I don't know. But she's keeping us on track, and that's all that matters."

Nelle smiled before pressing her hand to her now-healed side. "Let's get back to the wing."

"We're not going to talk about it?" my little sister said as we made our way to the aerie.

"Talk about what?" I asked.

"The fact that I'm seeing Aspen, and you can't keep your eyes off Laurel." She smiled widely at me, her black-tinted lips gleaming.

"Some things don't need to be discussed, little sister of mine. What we *do* need to talk about is the fact that you were hurt. I don't know if I want you moving around town as freely as you have been without someone around you to keep you safe."

She punched my arm and glared. "Oh, no, you don't. You don't get to be all caveman, big brother."

"I will if I have to be."

"No. You are the nice brother. The sweet cleaner who helps to fix the town and takes care of those around him. You don't get all growly and overprotective like a bear."

"So now you're saying there's something wrong with bears?" I asked, knowing I was annoying her.

"You're too much sometimes," she answered after a minute.

We made our way to the wing. Hawk shifters were like

some other shifters where we stayed together as a family grouping. But our clutch was smaller than the others. The bear shifters in the area had the largest pack of all the shifters. Ravenwood had some wolves, the jaguar, a few other shifter types, and the magicals. But we weren't like other shifters groups in that we tended to remain insular from others who were not hawks. I was usually the lone exception since I worked within the town's limits, cleaned up the magical messes, and my best friends were bears and witches.

We moved around the world, found other hawks like us, and found our mates. I wasn't exactly like them, but I *was* their leader. However, not everybody appreciated who I was or how we functioned.

Nelle and I made our way through a copse of trees, and I tapped on my shoulders as Nelle rolled her eyes and jumped onto my back, clinging like a little monkey.

Unlike the bear dens set in the forest and the cave systems, the wing was aboveground—*way* aboveground.

Our trees were immense, taller than any in Pennsylvania. But the magic of our wing and the Ravenwood coven meant that we could hide trees as tall as the redwoods that resided in the Pacific Northwest within our lands. And our tree houses and nests were located in their branches. It made it harder for others to find us and maintained our privacy.

Some of the wing didn't drive cars. They didn't even visit the town. Everything they needed was here, and they spent much of their time in their hawk forms because of it.

As shifter hawks, we tended to be two to three times as big as regular birds of prey, and our homes were quite large.

Hence the need for the magic and the trees that were out of this world.

"Is it weird that this smells like home, much like beneath the sea does?" my little sister asked.

I shook my head. "I don't think it's weird at all. You are of both worlds."

"And sometimes, I'm of none," she whispered. I hated that for her. Not everybody in the clutch agreed that Nelle should be allowed to stay in the aerie at all because she wasn't full-blooded. Not that they had any say in it. They were old school and preferred to mate within their species. That meant, once they found their mate, if they were in a different part of the world, they moved there and didn't look back.

I wasn't like that. My family wasn't like that.

And that was why my staying here as wing leader wasn't always the easiest thing. It had only been a week since the last challenge, and I was exhausted. But those under my command, my second, kept the peace while I tried to maintain our connection to Ravenwood. Because what others didn't understand was that the connection was what kept us safe. I didn't think there would be another direct challenge as there had been recently, but there might be something a little more subtle if I wasn't careful.

We wouldn't be able to make it alone. Not as the world evolved, and technology made it so only magic could keep us safe. Not with the eyes of humans who now saw far too much on us.

"Nelle?" my mother asked as she came down a rope ladder. "Why do I smell blood? What happened?"

"The revenants can swim," I said. After a moment, my mom let out a curse before going to help her daughter clean up.

"Can we talk later?" my mom asked. "I'm heading below the surface soon to undergo some peace talks with Nelle's father. But we need to talk before I go."

I nodded before looking at my second, Aiden, and my third, Colton.

"Are you okay?" Aiden asked.

I nodded again. "I'm fine. There weren't that many of them. But it likely means another necromancer's out there."

"Another witch ruining something else," Gerald, an elder, muttered as he walked past. I held up my hands when Colton started to snarl.

"They defy you."

I set my jaw. "They don't like that we're so immersed in the town business these days."

Aiden narrowed his gaze. "And they don't like that

you're spending so much time, at least according to them, with a special distraction."

I sighed, but they were right. The *distraction* wasn't my best friend. It wasn't the coven. And we all knew it. The distraction was my mate. The woman I loved but was afraid would never love me back the way I needed her to.

The wing hated Laurel. Not because she was a witch, and not because she couldn't control her powers, but because she was my mate.

And yet, she could never be mine.

Not unless something changed, or I burned right alongside her.

CHAPTER
THREE

Jaxton

The flames beckoned and I told myself it had to be a dream. This couldn't be real, yet it was all I could smell, taste, hear, feel.

The scents of burnt flesh and wild oak turned to embers surrounded me. The taste of ash was on my tongue, my lips, scraping down my throat. The sound of the flames as they shrieked and flickered and crackled and burned was nearly deafening—the feel of heat and yet of...nothing.

Because Laurel wasn't here anymore. I couldn't feel her. She was gone.

Turned to ash. A memory. A pale specter of the woman she had once been.

The curse had taken us all, yet it had taken her first and with every ounce of her being.

Laurel was dead. Gone. Burned.

I hadn't been enough to save her.

I woke with a shout, telling myself that it was only a dream and that I was here and whole. That I wasn't in pain.

That this wasn't the end.

And yet once I woke alone in my giant bed in my aerie, I knew that what I'd seen might be my future. I'd be destined to sleep alone, to be alone, to lead a people who judged me for the person I loved.

One I could never be with because she couldn't save herself, and I couldn't save her either.

I ran my hand down my face, ignoring the sweat-slick skin that ached. I'd had this dream before. Far too many times. Even more so since we'd lost Trace.

I still couldn't believe that one of my best friends, the man I'd thought might be the lynchpin for Laurel and me, was gone.

I'd loved Trace more than a brother, but we hadn't had a chance to find out if we could be anything more. The same had been true for Laurel, and a small part of me had thought that perhaps the reason none of us had completed the mating bond was because all three of us should have been with one another. In the end, I didn't think that was what would have happened. Trace had only ever been our friend. Always. Fate had decided that a triad wasn't in the cards for us, and now Trace was gone, and I had to find out exactly who I could be without him—and perhaps without Laurel.

It would be a fitting end, wouldn't it? If the two of them ended up finding their peace in the afterlife.

And yet, would there be peace if the necromancers came for us again? Faith had come for Trace after he died. She had turned him into a revenant, just like she had done with Alden, Trace and Rome's other triplet. The bear alpha, Rome, had been forced to kill his brothers again, and I hadn't even been there to help because I was taking care of the other revenants trying to attack the den and the town.

Faith, the necromancer who'd worked for Oriel, was dead now. We had seen her perish, and Sage had used her power to make it permanent.

I shook myself out of my reverie and got out of bed. I made it, fluffed the pillows like my mother had taught me, and went to shower. I was quick and efficient and didn't linger, mainly because there was no way I wanted to. Not alone, and not after that dream I'd just had. I needed to meet with the coven and the guys so we could make plans for what to do about Oriel and any other necromancer now working with him.

We didn't know who had sent the revenants the day before, but it had to be someone. Perhaps it was Oriel, or maybe it was someone else. The fact that we didn't know for sure worried me, but we would figure it out. We always did.

I pulled on a T-shirt and jeans and walked barefoot down the walkway to the shared part of the aerie.

People milled about, smiling at me and nodding, others giving me odd looks. I didn't blame them. After all, they didn't trust me. And why would they? I was only their wing leader. Sure, I had nearly died to protect them multiple times, but because I couldn't find a mate within the wing, and it seemed my mate might be a witch who couldn't control her powers, the people I protected didn't trust me. Laurel wouldn't even allow herself to think about the fact that we could be mates. And yet, my wing did. Often. What exactly did that say about the promise of what couldn't be?

"Jaxton!" Aiden called as he ran up to me.

I turned, my senses on alert at his tone. "What is it?"

"Our healer needs you."

I ran, following him along the rope bridges and up the ladders. We were up in the trees, so high that even other shifters couldn't find us. We had made an intricate neighborhood within the canopy, one I was proud of, even if it scared some of the four-legged shifters.

"It's Bliss. She's having trouble with the baby."

I cursed under my breath, my heart beating faster as I ran.

Bliss was one of my wing members, a small-in-stature

hawk shifter with a sweet smile and a tender disposition. She was nearing the end of her pregnancy, but I was afraid that it might be too early for labor.

I cursed under my breath and made my way to the healer's home.

Carol, our healer, knelt in front of Bliss as the younger hawk and her mate lay on the bed. Carol looked over her shoulder at me, her eyes filled with determination. Not fear, not anger, but *determination*.

And that worried me more than anything.

"I hear we're about to have a new baby hawk with us," I said, keeping my voice nonchalant. The scent of fear radiated through the home, and I told myself that as long as I remained calm, the emotion would travel down the bonds that made us a wing. Both Bliss's and her mate's shoulders began to relax marginally as I moved closer. It wouldn't be enough, but it would help some.

"Do you need my power?" I whispered to Carol, even though the others would be able to hear me. We had shifter senses, after all. And during childbirth, both Bliss's and her mate's hearing would be hypersensitive.

"Please," Carol said, and I put my hand on her shoulder, pushing power into her. The bonds that connected us flared, and they allowed her to reach for my wing leader power so she could heal Bliss and bring this new life into the world.

Sweat broke out on Bliss's and her mate's foreheads, the same with Carol's, and I put my hand on Bliss's knee for a second, squeezing and infusing her with power before I reached out for her mate.

He nodded and gripped my hand, and I knew that he would feed the power to Bliss through the mating bond, as well. That way, there weren't too many people in Bliss's line of sight, and she could focus on birthing the baby.

There were screams, tears, and much pleading to the gods before finally, the sweetest sounds in the world hit my ears.

A small cry and some watery laughs. Soon, a new baby hawk was in our wing. The hatchling wouldn't be able to shift for at least another year or two when she became a fledgling. She was so small, but she had big lungs and the tiniest hands I'd ever seen.

"Hold the new member of your wing, Jaxton."

"I can do that."

I held the baby to my chest, even before we gave her to her mother and father. This littlest wing member needed a bit more energy, some extra kick to make sure she would be okay.

Bliss and her mate looked at me, clearly worried but with pride, as well. I would soon give them their child, and they would be okay. But first, the baby needed a little bit of wing leader bonding.

She cuddled against my chest, making cooing sounds as I infused her with energy and the knowledge that she would be whole and cherished.

Carol worked on finishing with Bliss, and soon, the

new baby slept peacefully in my arms. I gently handed her off to her mother.

Bliss and her mate cried, giving me thankful looks. I walked away without another word, knowing I needed another shower, but it had been worth it. Our wing had a new member.

Nelle stood outside the door, pacing. When she looked at me, her eyes got wide. She beamed and threw her hands up into the air. She didn't scream or shout since nobody wanted to wake a sleeping baby, but everyone saw the joy in her face. I nodded my head and grinned.

"I would hug you, but you need a shower."

"Thanks for that." I cursed as I looked down at my watch and sighed. "I'm going to be late."

"You did good, big brother." Nelle rose on her tiptoes, kissed me on the cheek, and pushed me towards my house. "Go shower. I will make sure that people don't bother the baby."

I rolled my eyes. As did Aiden. Nelle technically wasn't a wing member and couldn't tell anybody what to do, but most people still listened to her. She looked intimidating with her goth outfit, leather, and chains, though I thought she looked adorable. Not that I would ever tell her that because she would likely kick my shins hard with those steel-toed boots.

I quickly showered again and made my way over to the town center. We were meeting at Rowen's shop, the witchy tourist shop, Into the Wood. It was all about spells, witch lore, and helpful for the paranormals and those still learning what and who they were. Tourists also came, but they only saw what Rowen wanted them to see. That was why she was attached to the town wards as she was. She and her new coven would ensure that the humans didn't find out what went on with the paranormal world inside Ravenwood.

I knew that she needed help, though. Doing it on her own was too much. Sage helped how she could, but the water witch was still too new to do some of what Rowen needed.

We all knew that. And yet, Rowen kept acting as if she could handle it all on her own.

I knew Laurel wanted to help. She wanted to work on spells and connect her life force to the town as Rowen had. But she couldn't. Every time Laurel used magic, she got one step closer to having it be the last spell she ever did.

I didn't want that to happen. I knew it couldn't. My hawk anchor slid over my body, agitated at the thoughts whirling in my mind.

I knew Laurel needed to try the spell that Rowen had found that we hadn't tried yet. Only I was afraid it would be too much for her. The more I pushed, the more she pulled. I wasn't sure what we were supposed to do.

I walked into the shop and found that I was the last one to arrive. Rome and Sage were looking over a book, the big bear protecting his mate no matter where he went. He was Trace's identical triplet, and every time I saw him, it was like a kick in the gut. Even though I never confused the two when they were together and always knew who my best friend was. Now, Trace and Alden were both gone, and seeing Rome reminded me of what had been lost. I could only imagine how Rome felt every time he looked in the mirror. Hence why we didn't talk about it.

Ash stood in a corner, studying a stack of books as if he hadn't a care in the world. I didn't know why he was here. Considering the curse, I didn't know what Ash felt. Or even if he *could* feel.

Rowen sat at a big table in the back, frowning as she studied another book and did her best not to look over her shoulder at Ash. Ash did the same with her.

Since I wasn't one to talk about not looking at a certain person, I didn't say anything.

Laurel stood the closest to me, her chin raised. "About time you showed up."

I didn't sigh, I just gave her a look. "Bliss had her baby. I needed to stay."

Laurel's eyes widened. "But it's too early. Is she okay?" She moved forward and put her hand on my arm. I did my best not to jolt at the touch, the sensation of her skin on mine. My hawk pushed at me, wanting her. It wanted to secure the bond we should have had years ago but didn't. I just stared at her, then looked down at where she touched me. She squeezed my arm once, the touch nearly too much for me to bear, before letting go.

"It'll be a harder road than it should have been, but the baby will be fine. Bliss and her mate are doing well. Nelle is making sure that visitation hours are adhered to."

Laurel smiled at the dryness in my tone. "If anyone can handle them, it's Nelle."

It didn't matter that Nelle was part of the mermaid clan and not my wing. She was a force of nature. Though not everyone in the wing liked her around due to their prejudices, Nelle was stronger than their hatred. And I threatened anyone who came after her.

"Do they have a name yet?" Rowen asked as she stood, wiping her hands on her black linen pants.

I shook my head. "No, but I'm sure Bliss and her mate will want the world to know when it's time."

"We'll have to make sure we do a spell when it happens to welcome the new little one into our town."

Sage beamed at Rowen's words. "Can I help?"

Rowen gave Sage a warm smile. "It's for our coven. Of course, the two of you will help."

No one else looked at Laurel as Rowen spoke, but I noticed how she stiffened. Rowen still considered Laurel part of the coven, even if Laurel didn't.

And I wasn't sure I could fix any of that.

"Now that I'm here, I guess we should get started. Again, I'm sorry for being late."

"No need to be sorry. You helped welcome a new life

into the world." Rowen let out a breath, her gaze going distant, but I didn't ask why.

Sage beamed up at Rome and then leaned into him. The two were newly mated, and we were dealing with a war at our doorstep, but I wasn't sure that Sage or Rome wanted to wait too long before welcoming a child of their own.

The thought of a little bear cub with possible magic made me smile. The couple would be good parents and would probably know what they were doing. I, on the other hand, felt like I was floundering. Maybe that was because of the woman who stood next to me at the moment.

"We still don't know who sent those revenants," Ash whispered.

Rowen stiffened for a moment at his voice, but then she nodded, forcibly relaxing her shoulders. "No, we don't. While we can assume it was Oriel, it could have been any member of his team. Or even another necromancer who wants our home and the power within its wards."

"Do you believe Oriel has a team?" I asked.

Rowen pushed her hair away from her face. "He had Faith. He could have others."

I leaned forward. "And if he does, then we need to figure out who they are. If they're necromancers, then we need to determine what other magic they have."

Necromancers were witches who turned bad. And

since witches were elemental by nature, they all had an element they leaned towards. Faith's had been water, much like Sage.

"It's fire," Laurel cut into my thoughts. We turned to her. "That fire you felt before? That wasn't me."

I believed her, but I wasn't sure the others did. I reined in my anger at that.

"It didn't come from Laurel," I added. When the others nodded, Laurel grumbled.

"Excuse me. I told you before it wasn't me. Just because I don't use my magic because of what it does to me, doesn't mean I lost all control and let fire come from a totally different part of the lake from where I was standing. I wasn't even in that direction. Therefore, it couldn't have been me. And if you thought beyond the fact that you're so worried about what my magic could do, you would realize that."

Rowen held up her hand, air magic sliding over us all.

I scowled at her.

"You're right. We're sorry." She looked at the others as they nodded and then gave us a tight nod. "However, if this necromancer *does* have fire as their element, that means you are our best person to fight against them."

"You know I can't do magic," Laurel said at the same time I spoke.

"She can't do magic."

Laurel scowled at me, but I just raised my chin, defiant.

"We know that," Rowen said and then shook her head. "But we still need to try."

I ignored the sense of loss that loomed over me as we continued planning, deciding what might be coming and trying to figure out how to stop it.

AFTER THE MEETING, my shoulders tense from the lack of knowledge of anything going on, I went back to my task of cleaning up any messes the supernatural left behind. My job was to make sure the humans didn't find out what was going on in Ravenwood. Rowen worked her own magic with the wards, and I did what I could with what was left.

I nodded at Aspen as he passed me on the street and held back a scowl. I didn't know what was going on between him and my sister, and I wasn't sure I liked it whatever it was, but it wasn't my place to get involved. At least for now.

The man returned my nod regally before walking down the sidewalk as if he weren't the leader of a secretive race of supernaturals that even shifters didn't know much about.

I cleaned up glass from a broken window, helped a teenager out of a sticky spot, and then shifted and raced our jaguar friend down a path, just to see Frank smile.

When he won, I grinned, shook my head, and made my way back to my home just as darkness settled in.

I walked inside, stripped off my shirt, and was about ready to take my third shower of the day when I froze, a familiar scent filling my nostrils.

It wasn't a dream this time. It couldn't be, I was awake. I turned to see Laurel standing in my home.

"How did you get in here?" I asked.

"I know how to climb." She shrugged, and I held back a smile. She was right. She used to climb through my window up in the aerie when we were teenagers, both of us not knowing enough about each other yet knowing too much at the same time.

"What are you doing here, Laurel?" I asked, trying not to make my tone sound accusatory. I liked her here. I wanted her here always. But she couldn't be. Still, I needed to know why she'd come.

"You were right, Jaxton." She swallowed hard. "It's time."

Suddenly, the world felt as if it were falling around me, her voice echoing in my head.

It was time.

Time for death.

FOUR

Laurel

My hands shook, but I felt that was a common occurrence these days. I didn't know if it was from the pain that constantly radiated through my veins or the tension from the worry of what might come later.

I tried to ignore it. Tried to tell myself that I would find a way to survive. But I knew that wouldn't be the case.

This afternoon, once Rowen finished collecting the materials for the spell, we would try to break the curse.

Not the whole Christopher curse. That was something

Ash would have to do to unravel himself. However, *my* part of the curse might have a solution.

Sage had found it. A small line in a book about a spell that could douse the flames of the unworthy. She had scowled at it, but I had come closer. Wondered if I was the one who didn't possess the worthiness to continue as part of the coven. Rowen had merely given me a look and then went to search for the spell the note had spoken of.

Did my best friend think I was unworthy? Or was Rowen just following along with what I had said? I wasn't sure, but maybe there wasn't a choice in what needed to happen next. Because here we were, about to perform a ritual—and I could die.

That was the outcome of this spell. I would die, and then I would be reborn without the Christopher curse. I would burn from the inside out, but it would be my choice this time. My flames coming into existence to purge.

And I wanted nothing to do with it. Only, if I didn't do this, I would still die. I might as well *try* to find a way out of it. To make it out alive to protect the town and those I loved. I needed to determine who I needed to be and find the strength and the power to become that person.

Jaxton wanted me to do this. He wanted me to survive and find a way. But to what? To be with him? Or maybe just to be.

He was the one who'd told me it was time. I couldn't spend another moment waiting for something to come to us without trying. It had been years of me nearly dying, of burning from the inside.

"Are you ready?" Ash asked. I turned to him, trying to relax at my brother's tone.

The man in front of me wasn't the boy I had grown up with or even the man I'd come to know before everything changed.

I missed the Ash he used to be, the one from before the curse.

I wasn't sure when that Ash might come back or if he could, though I knew he had to. For us to defeat the darkness, we needed to be a full coven, and Ash was a witch. He wielded earth. Had rocks and dirt that created a magnificent mosaic on his skin and acted as his anchor. A tattoo that told us who he was.

He was still that, even if a part of him might be forever gone.

I hated that I had lost a piece of my brother. And I wasn't sure how we were supposed to fix it.

I only knew that we needed to.

"I don't know if I'm ready," I said after a moment, finally answering him.

"You don't have much of a choice. You were right when you said it was time. Time to stop waiting to see if this might work." He frowned at the notes he'd taken and rubbed his hand over his chest. I froze at the gesture, wondering what it meant. But then he looked down at himself as if he hadn't realized he had done it and dropped his hand.

It had been his heart. A place that had to be empty because of what resided within him—or rather, what didn't.

And yet it ached? For who? For what?

Or was I once again reading too much into things?

"We will make the connection together and bond as brother and sister. That should enable you to reach out and find that person, *me*, once you return to us."

What he didn't say was that, once I was done burning to let the curse take hold, I would be able to reach out for the bond I had with Ash, our sibling bond, and find a way to live once again.

I would die today so I could rise again. So I could break the curse and become one with the coven.

It was the only solution we had been able to find. The only way that might work. But I didn't know if it would.

"You're sure this is going to work?" I asked, swallowing hard. "Will you be able to do your part on the other side of the bond?"

I didn't tell him that I was terrified. Because of his curse and what had happened to him, I wasn't sure we would be able to bond the way we should. I might end up killing him in the process.

"It should be fine. After all, we've been bonded since birth. We're siblings. Family."

He was saying the words, and yet, somehow, they

didn't ring true. It wasn't that he was lying to himself or me. It was just that he was who he was now. Changed.

Everything was wood and stone; not the Ash I used to know.

Today, I would be the one burning to ash even while he had the name. I'd always found it ironic that I had been born after him, my fire power fully intact, while he had been named for the result of fire itself.

"It would have been better if you'd had a mate for this. A true mating bond is stronger than a sibling bond. But with Trace gone..." Ash began and then stopped speaking after I let out a pained gasp.

"Did I say something wrong?" he asked. I could sense that he was apprehensive. Worried. Ash may be different now, the curse twisting him up inside, but he didn't want to hurt those around him. He wasn't casually cruel. He was simply honest to a fault, even with his secrets.

"Trace wasn't my mate, Ash. At one point, I thought it would have been nice if he were, but he wasn't. The bond would never have formed between us."

Ash tilted his head, studying me. "Is there someone else, then? Someone you can create a mating bond with to make this work?"

I swallowed hard. "I don't know."

"Jaxton, maybe? Perhaps Jaxton should stand with me, and you should try to create a bond with both of us. Use the sibling bond and a potential mating bond to come back. To find a way back to both of us."

I winced and pulled away. "It doesn't work like that, Ash."

"I'm aware that mating bonds don't always work the way you want. When you take that step, things can be irrevocably altered to the point where you can't come home. I understand that. You know I do."

I turned on him, pain radiating through me. Of course, he knew. He was who he was because of the decisions that had broken him. Those that had broken Rowen.

"I think we can just work with you."

"No, we won't," Jaxton said from behind me. I turned, my hands shaking.

"How long have you been standing there?" I asked.

How long had he been listening? I hadn't even noticed he was there. Ash and I stood in Rowen's store, waiting for the others, and Jaxton had walked right up without me noticing.

"He's only been there for a short while," Ash answered.

I rolled on my brother, glaring. "And you didn't let me know that he was listening in?"

"I was invited here, Laurel," Jaxton said. "I can't be listening in or eavesdropping if I'm supposed to be here. And, apparently, I'm truly supposed to be here."

"It's not you. I could kill you, Jaxton..."

"But you don't care that you could kill yourself? Your brother?"

I threw my hands up into the air. "That's not what I'm

saying. This can't hurt Ash. Not the way it could hurt you."

My brother couldn't lose what he didn't have. And that was why he was the perfect person for this. Ash was strong enough to come back from whatever we threw at him today. What the bond we'd use for the spell would attach to—if it could at all—couldn't break him.

Jaxton's eyes narrowed, his anchor tattoo sliding over his body like a whirlwind. "You weren't going to tell me that you were going to risk everything, even though I was the one pushing you towards this ritual? You weren't going to tell me that I could help?"

I swallowed hard, fear clenching my heart in a punishing grip. "You can't help, Jaxton. We both know that."

"You and I need to talk. Before this happens."

"I think we're out of time," Rowen announced as she walked in, looking between the three of us as Sage and Rome followed her.

"What's happening? What's going on?" Sage asked as she moved forward.

"I think a conversation that should have happened long ago is finally taking place," Rowen grumbled.

I glared at my best friend.

Rome grumbled low, letting out a deep chuff that was all shifter. "Stop it."

"What?" I glared at the bear.

"Stop it."

"Stop what?" Rowen asked. "Stop talking about what all of us are ignoring?"

"You and Jaxton could be mates. I once thought it could be you and Trace—and maybe it could have been, or maybe it was the three of you. I don't know. But my brother is gone. Both of my brothers are." I heard the growl in Rome's voice, and I ached for him. I wanted to help, but there was nothing I could do. Instead, Sage rubbed his chest, and he pulled his mate close. "I almost lost my mate once—more than once, if I'm honest. I lost my brothers. I'm not going to lose my friends. We know that the town is cursed, and that the Christophers were cursed more than once."

"And it's my family's fault," Sage said.

I shook my head. "It's not your family's fault."

"I know the story," Sage said, raising her chin. "The youngest Prince daughter, the family who founded this town, was in love with a Christopher. But he didn't love her back. So, when she broke in grief, her power lashed out at the Christopher line—albeit unknowingly."

I looked at her, then at my brother. "And from there, no line shall be whole, and all those who fall shall burn or fade," I repeated the long-ago curse. "I know it. I am the burn."

"And I am the fade," Ash whispered.

Rowen's jaw tensed as he spoke. I hated this for them. I loathed that our family line was severing because of a long-ago curse that had been an accident.

Even accidental magic had strength. And after centuries of twisted magic and power and curses, our family was finally running out of time.

"If we are mates..." Jaxton began, his voice hollow, "if we are mates, then let me help." I froze.

"We don't have a bond." I couldn't let him die. I didn't want to hurt my brother, but he could survive. If I burned, our bond wouldn't break him like it would Jaxton.

"But we have the potential. You can't deny that. Ash and I could do this together. We can both be your focal point so you can come back."

I shook my head. "It could kill you."

"That's a risk we're both willing to take," Ash whispered, and Jaxton nodded. "You know this, Laurel. I know you're afraid of hurting us. I know you worry what could happen. But I am more afraid of what might happen if we don't try."

I looked at all my friends, my family, and fisted my hands at my sides.

"If we do this, you could die." I needed Jaxton to understand that. I didn't want him to risk himself. Not for anything, but especially not for me. Didn't they see that? Couldn't they see what I'd needed to push away for so long?

"If we *don't* do this," Rowen snapped, "you will surely die. They're willing, and we are as well. Rome, guard us. You'll be the only one with strength after this."

The big bear nodded. "Of course. Should we get my beta? Your second? The others? Aspen?"

Rowen shook her head. "No, I feel it has to be the six of us." She looked at me then. "It's always been the six of us."

I gritted my teeth and nodded. "Fine. Fine."

Rowen barked out orders as my emotions whirled. I looked at Jaxton. "I don't want you to get hurt."

He moved forward and cupped my jaw. I hated that my magic reached out to him, wanted him. The anchor tattoo of flames on my side rolled around, moving over my chest and up to my neck, then over my cheek to touch Jaxton. His hawk tattoo, his anchor, flew down his arm and over his hand, so our anchors touched. The magic pulsated.

"Laurel. You know it's time." He echoed his words from weeks before, and I swallowed hard.

"You know I can't mate with you. Not truly. Not with the curse. It doesn't work that way. It only solidifies the curse further."

It had with Ash. That was one more reason I had never tried to find a bond with Jaxton.

The hawk nodded tightly, pain in his eyes. "It's the potential. I'll be here."

"As will I," Ash said. "It's not a mating bond, but a sibling bond can aid."

I wasn't going to win this argument, and a selfish part

of me was glad for the support. "Okay. Okay. I guess I don't have a choice."

"We don't," Sage whispered, her eyes filling with tears.

Rowen, Sage, and I stood in the center of the room, holding hands as magic pulsed around us. Jaxton and Ash stood behind me like pillars of stone as they waited for the magic to come.

"Rome will watch over us, keep us safe from any dangers from inside or outside forces. The three of us will say the words, cast the spell, and will push our magic into Laurel so she can let the curse unfold, let the flames engulf her. And when she comes back, both Ash and Jaxton will reach for her through the bond, and we will rise again as new."

It sounded insane. But this was the only thing that might work. It was the only thing that could.

I just had to hope it was enough.

I let out a breath and met their gazes, nodding. Ash gripped my right shoulder, Jaxton my left, and we began.

"*As flames and fire and energies rise, wing the magic across the skies. Take this witch we offer thee, purge her darkness so she can see. Open eyes and cleanse her soul, purify her magic and make her whole. When she rises and breathes again, the curse will be gone, the strife will end. From our coven, these three and three, this is our will, so mote it be.*"

Pain slapped at me, carving deep grooves into my skin. I screamed, nearly going to my knees, but the magic kept me upright. Flames licked at my body, scorched me from the inside out. Starting with my toes, it wrapped its way around my calves, running up my legs to my hips, my chest, down my arms, all the way to my face. I wasn't sure if anyone else could see the flames, but I could. A deep purple, a light blue, a scorching red, and a vibrant orange.

I was the flame. I was the pain. This was the end.

Both Jaxton and Ash let out grunts as I reached out to them, my magic trying to find any bond it could.

The curse was still there. It wrapped a mystical cord around my neck, twisting until I could barely breathe.

I heard people shouting, pulling at me, tugging at the others, but there was nothing I could do. I was dying.

This would be my end.

With an unyielding curse and a spell gone awry.

Tears slid down my cheeks and almost immediately turned to mist as they steamed away, the flames intensifying.

Jaxton held on, the same as Ash. As all three of us fell to our knees, I cried. Not for myself, because I knew this was my end.

No, I cried because Jaxton and Ash were going to die with me. We had been wrong. And there was no coming back.

I looked up at my sister witches as they reached for me, as they whispered spells to bring us back. Tried to save us. But it wouldn't be enough.

I would never be enough.

With a breath, Rome was there, his bear's roar loud enough to shake the windows. He pulled at Jaxton, and then at Ash. I screamed, the slightly weathered bonds between Jaxton and me snapping as the spell ended as abruptly as it had come along. After, I lay curled in a fetal position, smoke wafting off my skin.

Then Jaxton was holding me close as Rome and Ash went to the others. I looked up at them and tried to speak, tried to do *something*.

It hadn't worked.

The curse was still there.

I felt it.

I was still going to die.

I opened my mouth to say something, anything, but my throat ached too much.

"I'm sorry," Jaxton whispered as he wiped the tears from my face. Suddenly, he looked up, his shoulders tensing. "They're here."

I froze as well and looked over my shoulder as something barreled through the door and crashed through the window of Rowen's store.

The revenants had found us.

And I had weakened my friends to the point that I wasn't sure we would be strong enough to fight them off.

I'd killed my friends, just as I had nearly killed myself.

CHAPTER
FIVE

Laurel

Jaxton threw his body over mine as the first blade soared over our heads.

I pushed at him, needing him to be safe and not wanting to be the reason he got stabbed or maimed. Even with the pain radiating through my body from the spell and the curse, I could handle myself.

"Get off me, Jaxton. Let me help."

"You're hurt," he snapped, and I glared at him.

"All of us are weak from that ritual, but we can fight."

"She's right. Let her up," Rowen ordered, her hair blowing in a wind of her own making. That meant her powers were at the forefront. She may be tired from the ritual and spell, but she was ready.

I had to be ready, as well.

The ritual might not have worked, and I might die in the next instant from magic, but I was part of this coven, damn it. And I would show my family, the coven, and the enemy that I could do this.

Even if I didn't quite believe it.

"How are they getting through the wards?" I asked as I staggered to my feet, leaning heavily on Jaxton. He glared at me but didn't say a word. He wanted to keep me safe. I knew that, but there was no keeping me safe when it came to an all-out war and battle. That was something we would all have to deal with.

"They must have a strong necromancer with them. Oriel?" Sage asked, and Rowen shook her head.

"I'm not sure. We can talk about this later, can't we?"

"Deal," Rome growled as his claws elongated, and he roared.

The windows shook. I didn't know if he would shift, but if he did, it could only help.

I turned to the side where I had left my sword during the ritual, only to see Jaxton holding it out to me. My eyes widened.

"So now you want me to fight?"

"I'd rather you be safe, but if you are going to run headlong into something that could kill us all, you might as well be prepared for it."

I took the blade out of its sheath and stared at him.

"And you fight beautifully with a sword," he whispered. And then we were off, even as I tried to understand why he had said that and why it did things to me.

As the revenant came through the window, I moved forward, crushing a small pendant that had fallen off one of Rowen's shelves.

I didn't want to think about the damage being done at the moment or the fact that Rowen would have to clean all of this on her own. Every time a revenant broke through the wards on the heels of a necromancer, it told us that we weren't prepared. We weren't ready.

Or maybe that the powers that be wanted us to fight and prove that we were worth the power they had given us.

I hated that Jaxton's and Rome's job was to clean up after the paranormal. It used to be paranormal accidents that occurred because of shifters, fae, and witches with power all in one place. Now, it was to clean up after the dead that walked.

Necromancers used twisted magic. They could begin and end elements, but as they moved closer and closer to dark magic, their souls became rotted and wrong.

Eventually, they were able to raise the dead.

Lower-level necromancers could only raise flesh. Higher ones could do that but also control the spirits that walked among us.

Faith had been a lower-level necromancer, at least

from what we could tell. But given the magic that pulsated around us, we had a feeling that Oriel and perhaps others with him were the higher-level ones.

That was why we had used a spell to send Penelope away completely when she died. To ensure that she could never come back to be used by Oriel or any of his ilk. That was why we burned the bodies of those who perished amongst us. Why Trace didn't have a grave but a small sign that said he had once been with us—had been family and more.

All of that so the necromancers couldn't come after us.

They couldn't use those we loved to attack us.

I hated Oriel more and more because of it.

I hated the power that broke within us that told us that we couldn't be enough. That the world was changing, and we couldn't fight back.

Though we had used the spell to keep those we loved from being used as spirits and revenants, that didn't mean we could do it for every single soul in existence. There was a cornucopia of magic outside the wards, and Oriel could use so many spirits and bodies from outside the town while we could barely hold onto the magic we had.

We spilled out of the store, and I was grateful that we didn't damage Rowen's place as much as we could have. She had lost so much, just like all of us, and while we butted heads most days, I hated the idea that she could lose her shop. It was a place where we learned magic and performed our rituals. It was also Rowen's. A centerpiece of her magic. Not the only one, not the main one, but still one of them. And since Rowen needed all she could get, I didn't want to lose that.

The town pulled on the coven's magic, and as Rowen was the last Ravenwood in existence, it taxed her more than anyone.

I'd had to block off my connection to the town because with each moment that passed with them needing the wards, I nearly died. It tugged on my soul and burned me from the inside out. I couldn't give my life force to the town.

Sage didn't have enough strength in her yet, but she was learning. Just the minuscule amount Sage *could* give to the town, primarily due to her mating bond with the alpha of the bears, had saved Rowen's life.

Rowen had been fading in front of us, much like my brother had faded into his new existence.

And we hadn't been able to stop it.

But we could stop this. At least that was what I told myself.

"I put a ward around my shop," Rowen snapped as she used her wind magic to decapitate a revenant.

"And they still got through?" I asked, slicing through the closest revenant with my sword. The blade melted through flesh. I held back a grimace, thinking this particular revenant was far more decayed than some of the others I had fought.

It seemed that whoever was controlling these had brought them from a longer distance. That meant the spells and rituals we were using on the graveyards close to Ravenwood were working.

And yet, I hated that I was tearing through these souls. That one day, someone might recognize someone they loved as we had before.

We were desecrating these bodies, but we weren't the first.

And we wouldn't be the last if this necromancer had anything to say about it.

"With so much power, and to get through both wards, whoever's controlling these has to be part of a group."

"Why did you have another ward set?" I asked, slicing into another.

"Because I wanted to keep us safe while performing the ritual. Clearly, it wasn't enough." I heard the pain in Rowen's voice, and I reached out to her, only to stumble back as a revenant clawed at me. A hawk screeched overhead, and I looked up to see Jaxton coming forward, using his talons to rip out a revenant's jugular. I caught myself, collecting as much strength as I could, and cut off the revenant's head. My hands shook, my body ached, and I knew I wasn't going to last long. My magic wanted out. I wanted to fight how Sage, Ash, and Rowen were working together.

They were the power of three, not me. Not now.

Only I needed to help. Fire licked at me, but then Jaxton was there in human form, naked but glaring at me.

"No. Don't use your magic."

"Don't tell me what to do." I sliced out with my sword, stabbing the closest revenant as Jaxton shifted back to hawk form to fight again.

As a hawk, he was easily two to four times as big as any bird of prey I had ever seen. He could lift a human with one talon and fly around with ease.

He was beautiful in that form, all gold with silky feathers.

He had carried me once, just for the fun of it, and we had laughed and rolled on the grass. Then Trace had shown up, and the three of us had picnicked and just cuddled with one another. We had been each other's distractions, our salvations. And yet it hadn't been enough in the end.

Trace was gone, and I was sure I would follow him soon.

Where would that leave Jaxton?

I swallowed hard, pushing those thoughts out of my mind. I couldn't let myself think. I didn't want to because I was so afraid that if I did, I would hurt more than I already did.

"Your wards are still up. And while it's keeping the revenants away from the rest of the town, it means the others in our alliances won't be able to help," Ash said calmly, looking at Rowen.

I winced at my brother's tone, not because he sounded judgy—though he did—but because that was him trying to be helpful. He just wasn't good at emotions anymore, and I hated it.

Rowen glared at him and snapped her fingers, the wards falling, causing a burst of sweet pain against my skin. "We need to keep these out of sight of any humans that are around."

"There aren't that many tourists anymore." I sighed.

Sage nodded. "It's as if they know they need to stay away."

The sounds of fighting echoed through the back alley that led to the trees, and I kept fighting, slicing at those who came at us.

Other hawks and bears came forward, as did Aspen, the fae leader. His people were able to fight back the twenty or so revenants that came at us again and again.

I searched in the distance for who could be controlling them. The necromancer in command had to be close for this many.

Only I couldn't see who it was.

"We need to find the dark witch," Rowen said, echoing my thoughts. I nodded tightly.

A jaguar flew through the air over me, and I ducked as a revenant came forward. But Frank sliced through him.

The jaguar bit at the man's carotid artery before moving off to get to another.

I hadn't seen Frank move that fast in a while, but I did my best to ignore him, trying to focus in front of me. The more I got distracted, the more mistakes I could make.

Then Frank let out a yelp and hit the ground, blood gushing from his side. I ran over to him, kneeling to cover his wound with my hand and apply pressure.

"It's okay. We'll heal you."

He blinked up at me, pain in his eyes, and my magic burst free.

How dare they hurt this man? This sweet jaguar, who was only here to protect us.

He rarely shifted into his other form anymore because he was the only jaguar here and didn't like feeling alone. He only turned to his animal form these days to race Jaxton and see who was the fastest. And I knew Jaxton let him win.

Because the older man was sweet, a little crackly with us, a bit grumpy, but he was a fighter.

And this revenant had just tried to kill him.

My flames licked out over my sword, even as they burned my flesh from the inside. Jaxton was at my side in an instant, still in hawk form as we took down the closest revenant. And then he glared at me with his hawk eyes before flying over me to get the next one.

With the group of us, we were able to take the rest of the revenants down. I staggered next to Rowen, who was now healing Frank along with Sage. Blood trickled out of my nose, and then Jaxton was in front of me, kneeling naked as he glared at me. He took my chin between his fingers and snapped out, "Why did you use magic? You know you're not supposed to."

"Fuck you," I muttered, blood pooling in my mouth. He cursed again, and then something between us pulsated.

My eyes widened, and I knew.

It was the start of the bond, the one we had tried to create with the ritual. The bond that I thought hadn't occurred at all. But it was there, in its infancy.

He sent power along the bond, and I did my best to wrap my magic around myself. What if my flames danced along the bond and burned him?

I would never forgive myself.

He sent more magic, and I felt my power rising—not to attack but to heal.

I hadn't felt that in so long, and I wasn't sure what I was supposed to do. So, I leaned forward as Jaxton knelt in front of me, and I simply held back tears.

He was healing me, but I couldn't do anything for him.

"Did you see her?" Rome asked as he came forward, naked since he had just shifted from his bear form.

I looked between them and shook my head.

"See who?"

"The woman with the strawberry-blond hair and a black mask over her eyes."

"The necromancer?" Rowen asked as she soothed Frank's hurts.

"I believe so."

"So, there's another one. Officially. This wasn't Oriel."

I sighed and pulled away from Jaxton just enough, knowing that I needed to breathe, needed to get away from him. But I couldn't. Not yet. Instead, I sat there alone. Jaxton looked over at me as if trying to heal me more, but I blocked him. I ignored the hurt in his eyes, not wanting to take any more from him.

I had already taken too much.

And now, with another necromancer in the game, he needed all the strength and power he could have. All he could get.

And I couldn't be the one who stood in the way of those he needed to protect.

Frank had almost died today to protect me, and the others had tried to circle me, but they needed to focus on themselves, not me. If they hadn't been weakened from the ritual, nobody would have been hurt at all. Instead, they had used some of their power to protect me, to try to break this curse. And here we were, weakened, bloody, and outpaced. Outmatched.

I could not do this again. I couldn't allow them to lose everything because of me.

I would either find a way to heal and survive this on my own. Or I wouldn't.

I wouldn't let my friends die because of me.

I looked at Jaxton.

I wouldn't let my mate die because of me.

CHAPTER
SIX

Jaxton

Cleanup after the attack didn't take long. Ariel, the bear beta, had carried Frank off to the den where he could heal surrounded by shifters. He might be a lone jaguar and enjoy his time on his own, but he would heal faster in the company of other shifters and bear cubs, who only wanted to show how much they loved their Uncle Frank.

Rome and Sage had followed, the alpha and his mate needing to spend some time with their pack after everything had changed.

Ash had wandered off somewhere after ensuring that Laurel was safe. I wasn't sure if she could consider nearly dying and knowing that there was a time limit on the essence she had left *unharmed*, but that was as good as she would get for now.

Rowen had taken one look at her shop and kicked everyone out. I had offered to help clean up, knowing that it wouldn't be easy for her to do it alone, but she had shoved me out with the rest of them. It didn't matter that it was my job to care for her just like she cared for us. Rowen had wanted to clean up the mess the bastards had made alone.

I would come by later to fix whatever she couldn't get done. If she let me, that was. But she would just have to deal with it. I might not be part of the coven, and she might not be a member of my wing and clutch, but she *was* family. In the intangible spirit, that meant we were all family.

With everyone else occupied, that had left me walking Laurel back to her place. I had wanted to go to mine to check on my wing—and I would—but first, I needed to make sure the woman who should be my mate got home safely.

I always needed to make sure Laurel was breathing. That she was still with us and not in such immense pain that she couldn't handle it. However, now that there was something between us, something beyond the initial touch and needs that I always felt with her, we needed to deal with it.

But I knew she wanted nothing to do with it.

"Thank you for walking me home, but I'm fine now."

"I'm going to walk you inside."

"You don't need to."

"I'm going to check on your windows, the doors, check to make sure you're healed, and you're going to deal with it."

"When did you earn the right to tell me what to do?" she asked as we walked inside. I did as I said I would. I checked the windows and glared at her. "When I held your shoulder and felt the bond pulse between us."

"We're not bonded, Jaxton. You know we can't be."

I whirled on her, my hawk coming forward. "Because you say so?"

Her lower lip trembled, and I hated myself. "Because that's how it has to be. We're not mates, Jaxton."

"Because you were going to be mates with Trace."

She shook her head, even as pain cascaded down my body at the thought of what my words meant.

"That's not what I'm saying," she whispered.

"I miss Trace just as much as you do, Laurel. Don't you understand that? He was mine, just as he was yours."

She turned her head from me for a moment before looking back. "He's gone. He's never coming back."

I let out a breath. "I know. And I wouldn't want him to come back. Not after what we saw."

Tears filled her eyes, and she began pacing in front of me.

"How dare that bitch bring him back? He should've

been able to die in peace. Instead, she made him a revenant. And we had to watch him die *again.* Can they do it again? Can they bring him back over and over?" she asked, her voice breaking as she spoke.

I wanted to reach out and hold her but knew I didn't have the right. Not even as her friend. "They can't. You know that we protected his body. His soul."

"I don't know. Are we powerful enough to do that?"

I looked at her then, feeling her pain. "We have to believe we are. If not, what's the point of any of this?"

She threw her hands up in the air. "That's my question. What is the point, Jaxton, when I'm not even sure we can survive past where we are? How are we supposed to be strong enough to take on Oriel and his ilk when we can't even fix a curse?"

I didn't know where to start with that. Because if I let myself, I'd growl like Rome and slash anyone who came near Laurel with my talons. But I couldn't, so I had to find logic. It was the only way I could focus. "You mean a curse that's been in your family for generations? Of course, it's going to take time."

"I don't have that kind of time. Don't you understand that? I'm dying with each breath I take. And suddenly, I'm supposed to find a way to be okay with us?"

"You're asking *me* to be okay with this? With losing you?" I gripped her face, telling myself I needed to calm down and not do it in this way. Only why the hell was I waiting?

If this were truly the end, if she would indeed leave me soon, I needed to tell her. She should be able to feel it, yet we weren't truly bonded. We may not ever be bonded in fate, faith, and time.

And that was something I would have to deal with.

I cupped her face in my hands, needing her, needing the connection that wasn't truly there. Yet I could feel the beginnings of it—just a tiny ember before it turned into a large flame.

"Laurel."

"Don't, Jaxton."

I took the blow. I knew she was protecting herself—or rather, she thought she was protecting me. Because as soon as I said the words, I couldn't take them back. She would just have to deal with it.

"I love you, Laurel. I've loved you for years. We've danced around who we could be to one another and *how* we could be with one another. I love your strength, your mind, your soul, your beauty. I love every ounce of you. Even that stubborn tenacity of yours that pushes everyone you love away because you have this false sense of needing to protect us. And yet the only way we can ever protect ourselves is by protecting you and being by your side."

"Jaxton."

I shook my head, leaned down, and pressed my lips to hers. I needed her taste. I had always craved her taste.

We weren't new to one another. We had loved each

other before, even if we'd hidden what we wanted and needed and desired and craved.

She tasted of ash, flame, sweetness, and...Laurel.

I had loved her once, and I always would. We had been too young the first time we kissed, not knowing who we could genuinely be for each other. When the curse took effect, and later when my father died, we had pulled away. I had needed to become wing leader, and she had needed to find out who she was.

And all along, Trace had been there with us. Not ours, yet still *ours*.

I kissed Laurel harder, needing her taste. When I knew I would never stop if I continued, I pulled away, resting my forehead against hers, needing to breathe.

"Jaxton. Why did you do that?"

"Why didn't you stop me?"

I heard the tears in her voice, even with the anger that could have been directed at the world at the moment. "You can't love me, Jaxton. You know I'm going to fade. I'm going to burn up and die, and you'll be stuck here with one end of a mating bond and nothing else. I'm a bad bet. I've always been."

"You can't make that choice for me."

"Of course, I can," she snarled before she pulled away and began pacing again. Her anchor flared in blue on her body, running down her neck. It normally rested on her hip or between her breasts, but now the anchor wanted me to see it.

Flames danced in her eyes, and I knew she was in pain, the scars on her body intensifying with each movement. But I didn't tell her to stop.

I could never tell Laurel to do anything. I could try, but I would always fail.

"I'm going to die. This curse will take me, and I won't be able to save this town or do anything for the coven. I refuse to be the reason you die, too."

"So, you think that if we're bonded, and you die, I'll die right along with you? That's not how mating bonds work." She was so damn frustrating, even though I knew she was scared.

"I could hurt you. I could tear away parts of you. And you need to be strong not only for your wing but also for your family and this town. They'll need you when I fail the coven. Don't you understand?"

"It's not you who will fail. It's the curse that has plagued you for so long. It attacked your family and has dug its tendrils into you, clinging without ever letting go."

"Because a witch loved my ancestor. And when she couldn't have him, she broke."

I hated that damn history, the curse that threatened us all as it wrapped its prophecy around us. "She didn't do it on purpose."

"I know. I tell Sage that all the time. Yet I don't think she believes me."

"Do you believe it?"

"I believe that just like with my aunts, just like with

my great-grandmother, I will burn to ash, and I won't come back."

"They didn't burn, not like you keep saying you will."

"No, their internal organs just melted because they couldn't handle the magic. And I have even more power than they ever dreamed of. I might take out the town if I'm not careful."

I cursed under my breath. "That's not going to happen. We won't let it."

"And what are you going to do, Jaxton? We've already tried everything in our arsenal. The ritual we attempted today was our last bet. We were going to create a bond with my brother, who can't create a bond with anyone else because of his curse. And *you*. You stepped up and declared yourself mine when we hadn't made that choice."

"We made it long ago on that field. Just because we walked away when we did doesn't mean we can't go back."

"Doesn't it? You left because your father died, and I will always understand that. You needed to be the wing leader, and we were too young to realize what mates could be. I thought we had more time."

"We did."

"And now, we don't. Trace is gone."

I held back a snarl, not because of jealousy but because Trace was mine, too. "He's gone, but he's always with us."

"You say that, yet I'm going to be the one who joins him when I die."

"Stop saying that," I growled.

"I don't know what else to say. I can't be with you. Don't you understand that? Because when I'm no longer here, it will take something from you. Any bond we share will shatter, and it will attack you. It will lash out. What if the flames dance along the bond and burn you? What if I hurt your hawk or the bonds you have with your wing because we are connected? I can't handle the magic, Jaxton. I can't be part of the coven. I can't protect this town. I can't be with you. Don't you understand?"

"Laurel," I whispered, my heart breaking, shattering into a thousand pieces as I tried to collect each one as if to preserve it for a time that would never be.

I stepped forward and brushed my knuckles along her cheek.

"Please, go. I can't think when you're around."

"I can only think when I think of you."

"That was a stupid line," she muttered, and I snorted. The tension began to leak out between us, but not enough. Never enough.

"I love you, Laurel. You pushing me away right now because you're scared won't change that."

"I won't be your murderer."

"I'm not asking you to be my savior, either," I murmured before kissing her again. She leaned into me, tears rolling down her cheeks. The fact that they evaporated into steam as soon as they touched her skin concerned me, but then again, everything about Laurel concerned me. I leaned forward, kissed her again, and pulled away.

"We're not done."

"We never should've begun."

"I'm not going to count that as an attack," I whispered. "Because I love you. And we're going to find a way through this. Fate won't take you away from me."

"Fate took Trace."

I set my jaw. "Maybe Trace was never ours to begin with."

"Then maybe I'm not yours, either."

I shook my head and left, waiting for her to lock the door behind me. When she did, I shifted forms, leaving my clothes behind in her garden bed, needing to fly. To soar. Shifting into my bird form was easy, a breath because of the power within me. The wind fluttered under my feathers, and I caught a jetstream, letting the power of the town and the magic surrounding us seep into my bones.

Laurel was mine. And I wouldn't let a fucking curse or a necromancer or darkness or whatever the hell was coming at us take her.

Trace had been our best friend, and while we had joked that he had been our third, maybe he hadn't been. Perhaps he had only been the person to connect us.

I didn't know. Regardless, there was no bringing him back. He was gone.

And I'd be damned if I let anything take her from me. I landed on my aerie, walked inside, and pulled on some sweatpants. While I didn't mind walking around naked, there was always a time and a place for it.

Aiden, my second, knocked on the door as soon as I threw water on my face. I knew he had been waiting for me, likely on the lookout. I opened the door, and he walked in, a frown on his face. "What's wrong?"

"The elders are in a tiff."

"Why?" I asked, having a feeling I knew what it was about.

"Well, they're glad that Nelle's gone because they don't want to deal with the fact that our community isn't pureblooded anymore."

I growled. "Really? It's been how many years, and they're still on my little sister because she doesn't shift into a hawk?" My hawk pushed to the surface, anger radiating off me.

My second shook his head. "I didn't say I agree with them. All I'm saying is that the elders are creating their drama. It's what they do. They like their ways set in stone. The fact that your mother married the king of the merpeople doesn't sit right with them, and it never will. But screw them."

"I like the sound of that. Let's just ignore them. Maybe the problem will go away."

He met my gaze. "You know the problem will never go away, Jaxton."

I ran my hand through my hair and headed to my kitchen to find something to eat. "No. Because my little sister is never going away."

"It'll make things worse when she finally mates with the fae king." My hand gripped the edge of my refrigerator. "Let's not talk about that. I don't have enough strength in me to deal with that image."

"Fair enough. They're also mumbling about the fact that you're spending so much time with the coven and with a certain witch they do not want in their circles." I whirled on them. "They're going to say something about Laurel? The woman who has protected this wing as much as I have?"

"They're afraid you'll choose her over them."

"You know why I possibly would. And you know why she will never let me."

"I know why, and they know why, and they're bigots. However, they're scared. No one knows what's going on with those necromancers. And while we know that you are putting all your soul and energy into protecting this town and the wing, they're also greedy and selfish. And they want you to themselves. That's why you're wing leader. They want you."

"Well, they'll just have to learn to share. Because Laurel's mine."

"Did you complete the bond?" Aiden asked, moving forward, his eyes wide.

I shook my head. "Not exactly. But it's going to happen. I'm going to save her. We're going to save this town. And the elders will have to deal with the fact that we're not in the nineteenth century anymore. Plenty of wings and dens and packs have various members. We've never been pureblooded, and they need to realize that."

My second nodded. "Okay, then. However, you still need to come with me."

I frowned, tore off a hunk of cheese, and started chewing. "Why?" I growled.

"Because your aunt needs a hug."

I cursed under my breath, my stomach no longer needing food. I set everything back in the fridge and braced myself against it. "William's been gone for how long?"

"Long enough that we know he's not coming back. He's dead, Jaxton. You felt the bond break."

"But we never found his body." I knew I was merely hoping at this point, but I couldn't let myself believe he was gone. That was my problem these days.

"I think I'm too afraid that if we find the trail, it'll lead to the necromancers having him."

I cringed and turned around. "You're right. Okay. I hate that my cousin's gone. That whatever happened to him happened without our knowledge. But the bond is broken. I can't feel him within the wing. My aunt needs a hug? Then that's what I'll do. Because I'm the fucking wing leader. If my people need me, I will be there."

"You don't have to tell me. I know you're always going to put us before yourself. And it's about time you have someone to lean on when you do."

I watched him leave before I followed him, knowing that I was all talk—at least for now. Because I didn't know if Laurel would ever let me keep her. If she would ever let me have her.

Still, I had to try. I had to do something.

My world was fracturing around me, and I wasn't sure how to fix it. All I knew was that I loved a woman who I *knew* loved me back but was afraid to do so.

No matter. I would protect her. I would protect everyone I loved.

Or I would die trying.

SEVEN

Laurel

I sat cross-legged in Rowen's home, telling myself that this was absolutely normal, that I wasn't losing a part of myself.

It had been three days since the attack and the ritual. I still didn't feel like myself, but I wasn't sure I ever would, not when I knew that we were out of options.

The bonding hadn't worked, and our spell hadn't had the necessary strength. I liked to think we would find a way to make it be enough, but I couldn't see it happening.

"Okay, let's talk," Rowen said as she rolled her shoulders back.

"We're not going to be talking about my curse, are

we? Because I don't think I have it in me to do it anymore."

Rowen gave me a look, then shook her head before turning to Sage. "We are going to practice some different coven bonding spells. Not for your curse, but to keep us together."

"And if I can't help?" I asked, swallowing hard and ignoring the pain. This time, it wasn't only physical but an emotional blow because I couldn't help Sage in this new world of magic and wonder. I couldn't show her the goodness and the purity that came with this new world. Instead, I was the one left behind to show the pain and anger that came with it.

"You can watch," Rowen began. "You don't have to join us. In fact, I don't want you to join us unless you feel completely comfortable."

"Okay, I guess I can go over what I know. At least from a pain perspective. And feeling."

"That would be helpful," Sage added, frowning. "Any help you can give so I can make sure I learn what I need to so I can help the town wards and coven would be appreciated."

"I'm just sorry that I can't be much help other than that."

Sage scowled at me, and it was such a different look for her that I held back a smile. "You teach me to fight, to be strong, to be brave. Stop putting yourself down because your magic is different than ours."

"I like when you get a spine," I replied with a laugh, and Sage rolled her eyes.

"I'm mated to a bear. Of course, I learned about strength and spine."

Rowen raised a brow. "You had spine before you even stepped foot in Ravenwood, and you know it." She let out a breath as Sage smiled, and I warmed inside. Something that had nothing to do with the fire deep within. "This is going to be a simple summoning spell, one to bring forth a new day and to find the strength that we need to overcome the obstacles in front of us. The next spell we'll learn will be the one to push away those outside forces that threaten to cloud our minds."

I looked at Rowen then and remembered all the times we had done these spells and practices as children. Rowen had always been the coven leader, the *Ravenwood*. I was a Christopher, one of the founding families just like Sage was as a Prince, but the Ravenwoods were the true town founders, the ones it was named after. Rowen always had the most power, even though she leached most of it to keep us safe.

I'd always been in awe of her strength, the way she could face any obstacle head-on. And these two spells had been ones that I had learned at her side.

They brought balance to the coven and to the witch.

I wouldn't have to tug on my elemental magic to help. I didn't know if Rowen had done that on purpose, but knowing her, she likely had.

We each sat on the floor in a circle, our hands upturned on our knees as we closed our eyes, and Rowen began to speak.

"Strength of the day, strength of the night, give us strength, lend us light. New day at dawn, nightfall behind, bolster our powers and open our minds. From ward to ward and shore to shore, let perseverance spread, forevermore. Maiden, Mother, Crone are we. This is our will, so mote it be!"

Magic swirled around us, warmth, hearth, and steadiness seeping into my pores. Sage let out a little breath, a slight gasp of surprise, and I smiled, knowing that she was finding grounding in her world. Something that I searched for daily.

The flames began to intensify inside me. I ignored them and told myself that this was easy. As long as I pushed the fire away and didn't pluck at the elemental magic within me, I could continue this.

"It's like its own power. Almost a cleansing but not."

I opened my eyes to see Rowen smiling like a proud mama at Sage. "Exactly. It's not easy, but it will find a way to summon the energy that you need to focus on for the day. There are cleansing spells we can do, too, but we're not going to work on those today. Mostly because it needs a little more time for prep because of....circumstances, than we have at the moment."

I didn't know if she necessarily meant me and that I wasn't sure I could help. She didn't say it, and I didn't force it. To do a cleansing spell, you needed to push your elements because they ran through you to help ease the power. Since I couldn't rely on fire, I needed to avoid certain spells. Sadly, though, the ones that protected the town and helped Rowen not kill herself using too much would focus on that element. Meaning, no matter what I did, I would never be enough to protect my best friend. To protect anyone. I ignored the ache because I needed to. I couldn't focus on what I couldn't save. Instead, I pulled out the power I could and worked on the next spell.

"Banish now with spell and will. Banish now with spirit's grace. Banish now with magic's power. All that's wrong and out of place."

This time my magic tingled more than it should have, and I realized I hadn't been focusing. I let out a hiss, my fire rising. I tamped it down.

Rowen cursed and came to my side, gripping my hand. "Breathe through the pain. It's okay."

"I'm fine," I lied.

"You're not fine. You focus too much on the flames, and now they've come to find you."

"They always find me. They're always there. That's the problem." I pushed my power out, completing my part of the banishing spell, and let out a breath. "I'm sorry."

Rowen clucked her tongue at me, sounding like her late grandmother and not herself. "Don't be sorry. You're doing well. You're doing more than you have in a few years."

I gave her a sad look. I had stayed away from her and our coven for years because it had taken too much out of Rowen to keep me steady. Yes, it had hurt me. Yes, I had felt like I was losing with every breath. That if I kept casting those spells, I would die. But I had truly stayed away to protect my best friend. Because Rowen would give everything to protect us, and I couldn't let her sacrifice herself for me.

"Are you okay?" Sage asked as she leaned forward and gripped my hand.

"Look, I'm not dying yet, Sage. You don't have to worry about me."

Rowen glared. "Don't say things like that. You shouldn't have had to pull on your fire to complete that spell. Why did you?"

I gave Rowen a sad smile. "My magic *is* my fire. That's the problem. You have so much power with air, but you can separate the two because you don't have that never-ending pain. I don't have that ease. Everything hurts, Rowen. And that's my problem. I'll deal with it. I have so far. But I don't think I can help the coven as I should. I'll do what I can, but I may be more of a hindrance than not."

"Stop it. You are not a hindrance. You have never been," Sage insisted.

"Is that the case? Or is it only what we want to believe. You need the power of three to protect this town from the darkness. That is what the prophecy has always said. That our town is cursed by those who will come to get us. Our town will lose its wards, its power, its people if we're not careful. That has always been what our talents were cursed with. And yet, we are fighting back. We are doing our best. But I don't think I am supposed to be a part of that. I don't think I can be."

Sage wiped away a tear, and I swallowed hard, ignoring the steam rising from my skin.

"I need to go," I whispered.

"You are part of this coven. You are our sister. We are so close to finding a way to save you and this town. We will make it happen."

I looked at Rowen and shook my head. "We can try, and we can wish, but that might not always work."

And then I stood and walked away, my hands shaking as the smell of smoke drifted behind me.

I staggered out of Rowen's home, ignoring how it felt as if I were leaving everything behind. Everything had changed and twisted, and I wished there was a way to fix things. Only I wasn't sure how.

"Laurel?" I looked up at Jaxton.

"Were you waiting for me?"

He shrugged. "Maybe."

Warmth and anger radiated through me, and I pushed them both out, not wanting to inflame my magic.

"Really? You don't think I can handle it?"

"I'm here because I knew you were working on a spell

today. At least that's what Rowen said. I didn't know if you'd want someone to lean on afterward."

"Why are you so nice to me? I'm horrible to you."

He leaned forward and cupped my cheek. "You're not. You're a good person, Laurel. You just don't trust yourself."

"Maybe I shouldn't trust myself. Why are you doing this, Jaxton? You could get hurt. I don't want you to be hurt."

"I won't get hurt. But I'm going to be by your side. Always." He let out a breath. "Come on, let me take you home."

I sighed and leaned into him, hating that I did because I'd always been like this with Jaxton. Full-on trying to pull away because I was afraid of what might happen if I leaned too far. He was always sweet, caring, and could be growly if the need was warranted. He protected those around him. He protected *me*. But who protected him?

It used to be Trace. And Rowen. And I did my best, but I was always sure I wouldn't be the vulnerability. That my magic would backfire and hurt him instead of protecting him.

"I'm a bad bet. You know that, Jaxton."

"You're my bet, so you're just going to have to get over it. I'm not letting you go, Laurel."

I sighed and leaned into him again as he walked me home. I felt Rowen's and Sage's stares on my back as we left, and I knew I would have to tell them what was going on later. I wasn't sure what I was supposed to do. For now, I would focus on what I could, and that was the magic within me, and the hawk at my side.

He walked me home, just a short distance away from Rowen's. I'd always loved being close to Rowen, the fact that even when we were children, we could sneak out and visit each other. While Jaxton and Trace had been my friends as teenagers and beyond since we were figuring out who we were to one another, Rowen had always been there.

And when the full effects of the curse hit me, and I'd thought I lost it all, Rowen had still been there—even though we had pushed at each other and through the pain we hadn't been able to avoid.

Jaxton walked me inside, and I looked at him, brushing his hair away from his face. "I wish things were different."

"We'll make them different. I'm not signing your death warrant yet, Laurel."

That gave me a start, and I smiled. "I'm trying not to. Why do you think I picked up the sword? Why do you think I keep trying? I want Sage to be as powerful as she can, so Rowen isn't alone."

"Rowen isn't alone. She has Ash."

"We both know that she can't have Ash. The shifters are strong enough to protect their own, but maybe not everyone. Maybe not the town."

"The divinations have always said that it needs the power of the coven, yet I don't think it foresaw the second curse layer on top of it."

"I'm not counting you out. I never will."

He leaned down and kissed me, and I sank into him, hating how I felt.

"I don't want to hurt you," I whispered.

"Then don't." He kissed me again, and I wrapped my arms around him, needing him.

"We can't create a mating bond," I whispered.

"We won't. Just let me love you, Laurel," he whispered, and I sank into him, knowing that I couldn't say no. I had never been able to say no to Jaxton, and maybe that was part of the problem.

He had always been part of me—body, mind, and soul. I had pushed him away when I was afraid, and I was *still* afraid. With every ounce of my being. But I couldn't just ask him to leave. Not when this could be my last moment. It was getting closer and closer to the end. We were all dealing with the outside forces waiting for us.

But I wanted to be selfish, just for a minute. Just for a moment.

And so, I let myself be.

"Are you sure?" I whispered, fear in my voice that I hadn't recognized until it was too late.

He kissed me again. "Of course. I want you, Laurel. You're mine. Just let me love you," he repeated.

I nodded against him and then held him tighter.

His lips started at my jaw, kissing and caressing before he slowly moved me to the couch and lifted me onto the back of it. I let out a breath, then slouched against him as he kissed and bit my lips. His hands went to the hem of my shirt and pulled it over my head, leaving me in my jeans and bra. He licked his lips and stared at me. "You always were too beautiful."

"That's what you always say."

"Well, you always take my breath away."

His hand went to my side and gently caressed the edge of my burns. They healed quickly because they were magical, and the balms and creams that Rowen gave me helped. But they always returned. Sometimes, in different places. This time, it was on my left hip. When Jaxton's gaze went to them, I shook my head. "It's fine. You can't hurt me."

"I don't know if that's the case," he whispered before pressing a kiss to my neck, and then to my jaw, and then between my breasts.

I sucked in a breath, his touch sending magic through my body. But this time, it wasn't hot. It wasn't flames. It was warmth, yet something all Jaxton, the man I had always wanted and knew could be mine. But also the one I knew I could never have.

My anchor slid around my body, connecting with his on his hand before his hawk flew over his arm, around his neck, and to his other hand resting on my hip.

I giggled, and he grinned up at me. "Do you think all anchors work like ours?" I asked.

He shook his head. "I think we're special. They like each other, just like I like you."

"You say the sweetest things." I wrapped my legs around his waist and pulled him closer so his jean-clad cock was pressed against my heat. We both groaned, and then he bit my lip before undoing the clasp on my bra. My breasts fell heavily into his open palms, and he slid his thumbs over my nipples. I groaned as he leaned down and latched his lips to one turgid peak. We both groaned at the sensation, and I grew wet, needing him inside me.

It had been ages since I'd had him. Since I had allowed myself to be. And yet, this felt like the first time. As if we'd both been waiting for this moment.

I didn't know how this could be. How could I want him so much without knowing who he could be? Who we could be together?

He played with my breasts, molding them, sucking on them, and then he kissed down my belly, over my jeans, and grinned up at me.

The sight of his dark hair between my legs made me groan, and I helped him undo my pants as he tugged on my panties and jeans, stripping them from my body. I sat at the edge of the couch, clinging to the edge as he spread my thighs and stared at me.

"You're so fucking beautiful."

"Are you talking to me or my pussy?" I teased, and he

grinned before he leaned down and licked me. I saw stars, my whole body shaking as he sucked on my clit and spread me before him. He lapped at me, paying sweet attention to every inch of me. And when he speared me with two fingers, I came around him, my magic flaring.

But again, it wasn't the flame. It was the other essence of me, the part that was a Christopher witch, not an elemental wielder. My magic reached out for Jaxton's, and with whatever elemental magic he had, his hawk reached towards me, as well. He kept sucking at me, giving me exquisite pleasure before he stood and stripped down. I reached between us, gripping the base of his long, thick cock, and we both groaned.

"I need you. Please."

"You never have to beg, Laurel, all you have to do is look at me, and I want you."

"Good, now get in me."

He grinned and kissed me again. "We won't do the bond. Not tonight," he assured me, even though I heard the need in his voice. It echoed the desire in me. We couldn't. Not tonight. Not when we weren't sure what was coming.

I didn't know why I had denied myself for so long. Probably because I knew I should. If I really let myself want him, it would be too much for both of us.

I didn't know what would happen if he was bonded to me when this curse finally took me. I would regret it for the rest of my days in the abyss if I hurt him as the curse hurt me.

So, tonight, there would be no bond, even though I knew we both craved it.

I took a deep breath and held onto him as our gazes met. He slowly slid inside me, inch by inch.

He was thick, so thick that he stretched me, and the ache that came wasn't for magic but for man and need. He let out a groan and bit my neck, though not marking me as his mate. Instead, he just let out a shaky breath, and both of us clung to one another as I slowly adjusted to fit him.

"I forgot how tight you are," he mumbled, and I laughed.

"Oh, good, I'm glad you're trying to remember exactly how it was for us that first time when we were fumbling hands and too-wet mouths."

"We're not going to fumble today," he whispered and then he gripped my right hip. He put his other hand right under my left breast, and then he moved.

I let out a sharp gasp and arched into him as he pumped into me, the couch moving with each thrust. It would have been comical, and yet I could only think of him. I didn't care about anything else.

My powers latched onto his, claiming him in a way but not fully. We both knew what would happen if we did that, so we kept those parts locked away. And yet, all I could do was breathe and be.

I couldn't let myself love him. I couldn't let myself think that I already did. I could be with him at this moment, and maybe in the next. And when I squeezed my inner muscles, and he groaned my name, whispering sweet nothings that were everything in my ear as he came, I breathed into him, my magic flaring but not causing pain.

For the first time in my memory, my magic was pure and without pain.

Because this was Jaxton, my mate.

The one man I could never have.

CHAPTER

EIGHT

Oriel

O riel stared across his dining room, pleased at the final additions section.

Unlike some of his family, he had been raised to appreciate the good things in life. Whether it be the art itself or how it was obtained. This particular piece above the mantel was a lost Monet, one that others had killed to possess—he had done a fair share of it himself. However, his hands weren't too dirty for this one, not when he had other people to do that for him.

Now his dining room was complete, and as he enjoyed his well-done steak and sides, he figured it was time to see what he could do about a certain member of the Ravenwood community. He needed to destroy the coven. He needed to ensure that the prophecy came to fruition—at least, on his end. And to do that, a key player had to be removed. It had taken far longer than it should have to realize who the person was.

Faith, dear Faith had been wrong in her summation of the person's identity. Although taking Trace out had been important for Oriel's bottom line, it hadn't been the only thing.

No, the shifter had been important to the community and to the pack, but he hadn't been the lynchpin that Oriel had been searching for. Now, though, thanks to a very convincing battle, Oriel and his team knew who they were looking for.

"Would you like me to handle it?" Renee asked, and Oriel looked up at his lieutenant.

She sat next to her mate, the two of them smiling coolly at him. Their steaks were a little bloodier than his, but there was nothing like a well-done filet mignon. He couldn't stand the sight of flesh on his plate. It needed to be cooked. That was the only way to eat a filet.

He was a good leader and let his lieutenants eat however they liked instead of forcing them to eat what he wanted. At least, for now. He might change his mind later.

"Once we take out this person, it will be easier to dispose of the coven," he said after a moment.

Renee nodded, and her mate just stared as if he didn't

have an opinion. Oriel wasn't sure the other man ever did, but he would be essential in this particular part of the battle, so he wouldn't complain. He would take care of the man shortly. Or perhaps he would ensure Renee did it. That would probably be better. Having to kill one's mate would be a true sign of loyalty.

But first, they needed the shifter to do what Oriel wanted and take care of their little problem.

"Make it look like an ambush. Perhaps from someone he trusts."

Renee nodded. "We can handle that. He has more enemies than he cares to admit."

Renee's mate finally spoke. "The dissension in the ranks is enough that it won't seem like you, but rather those he has angered with his current predilections."

Oriel nodded, a smile playing on his face. "Good." They needed him out of the way to take care of the coven. And then, Rowen would be his.

He held up his glass of Bordeaux, and the others did the same. A cruel smile played on Renee's lips as her mate scowled at Oriel, but not in anger, that was just what his face looked like.

"To the end of the one in our ranks, and to Ravenwood and our making."

"To Ravenwood," they agreed and sipped their wine. Images of Rowen occupied Oriel's mind and a small smile appeared. The coven was within his grasp.

Those of Ravenwood had dared to take what was Oriel's, and now they would pay.

But first, they would know true pain.

They would know what they had caused.

Jaxton

I lay curled around Laurel, holding her close, pretending that this was how our day would be. That we didn't have to get up or do anything other than what we were doing right now. That we could remain here until the end of time, breathing, pretending that this was our life.

Only I knew that reality would creep in at any moment, and there would be no going back.

Laurel rubbed against me, still asleep, and I held back a groan. Her tight little body, with that firm little ass pressing against my already hard cock wasn't exactly a way for me to keep sane today, yet I didn't want it to stop.

What I wanted to do was lift her thigh and wake us both up in the best way possible. I knew she needed the sleep. And thus, making love again probably wouldn't be good for either of us. Because Laurel would walk away. I knew she had to. She wanted to protect me, and maybe even herself. And that meant I either had to be the one to keep her or let her walk away.

"You were thinking so hard, you woke me up," Laurel grumbled, and I swallowed hard, telling myself that as long as I kept still, she wouldn't be able to read the emotions on my face once she turned over.

Maybe that would be a lie, but I was never good at keeping things from Laurel. Hence why we were in this situation again.

"Sorry. I have a lot to think about."

She turned in my arms, our legs tangling as her naked breasts pressed against my chest. "I think we both have a lot to think about."

I cursed under my breath and then pushed her hair away from her face, cupping her cheek. "Laurel."

"I know. I know."

She leaned forward and kissed me gently. While I wanted to pretend that this was just the beginning of something far better for both of us, I knew that wasn't the case. I knew that this was probably goodbye. Perhaps there was always going to be a goodbye.

"Don't look so sad," she whispered.

"I feel like that's usually what I say to you."

"You should get going. We need to meet the coven later."

"We're just not going to talk about what happened then?" I asked as I sat, running my hands through my hair. The blanket pooled around my waist, leaving us both bare on top.

"I'm sorry."

"You better not be sorry about what happened," I growled before getting out of bed and shoving my legs into my pants.

"I know. I meant that I'm sorry I keep screwing everything up and don't know what I'm doing. I used to think I was better than this. Better *at* this. And now, everything is just wrapped around itself, and I can't find my way out. How are we supposed to find our way out when we don't even know who's attacking us or who's coming at us? Or even how to break this curse? It almost doesn't make any sense to me, and yet I know it has to. Because I hate hurting you. I hate watching you walk away."

I whirled at her. "You're the one who's always walking away, Laurel. It was always like that, even when we were with Trace."

And there it was. *We.*

Because we had both thought Trace was ours, and we had been wrong.

So fucking wrong.

"I thought he was ours, too, but he wasn't. He was just our steppingstone. No, that's a horrible thing to say. I didn't mean that." Her hands went to her mouth for a moment before she let them fall.

I moved around the bed and cupped her face before crushing my mouth to hers. She leaned into me. "I know. I know you didn't mean it like that. But Trace *was* part of our past, and I thought he would be part of my future. I thought you both would be."

"And now I'm dying, too," she said woodenly, and he held back the scream of rage threatening to erupt.

"Trace wasn't ours, even if we might have wanted him to be," she whispered. I lowered my head to hers, trying to catch my breath.

"And because he wasn't ours, we have to somehow move on and figure out our lives without him."

"I just don't want you to have to figure it out without me."

"Then stop saying that. We'll find a way."

"How?" she asked as she stood and went to put on her clothes. "How exactly are we going to figure that out? We haven't yet. I almost killed you and my brother trying to figure it out, and it hasn't worked out yet."

"We can't just give up."

"You don't think I'm trying? If I gave up, I would just spark my magic and let myself burn. But I haven't. I'm sitting here, and I'm fighting. I'm trying to protect this town. You. Everybody. You know, if things were different, I wouldn't run the way I usually do. And I wouldn't be trying so hard."

"If things were different, we wouldn't feel like this curse was for us specifically, and not just the town."

She gave me a look, and I sighed.

"I don't want you hurt any more. I want everything to go back to some sense of normal. But then I remember we don't have a fucking normal."

"We don't. And I don't know when that's going to change. I need time, Jaxton."

I gave her a look and sighed. "What if we don't have that kind of time, Laurel?" I regretted the words as soon as I said them as she blanched. "Laurel," I started again.

"No, you're right. We don't have that kind of time. But I still need it. I... I care about you, Jaxton."

I hated that phrase, but I knew she couldn't say *love*, not when we didn't know what would happen next. So, I had to let her get away with that.

For now.

"I'll give you time, Laurel," I whispered. "But not too much."

She smiled softly, and I leaned forward and kissed her gently. "I won't take too much time."

I picked up the last of my things and left, knowing Laurel needed space. And maybe so did I. We hadn't slept together in years, even if the two of us had been prowling around each other for what seemed like our entire lives. I had loved her every moment I had known her, even if that love had begun as one thing and changed into another. I'd loved her when I thought she was Trace's, and when I thought she was mine.

And I would love her until my dying day.

I just didn't know what I was supposed to do without her.

The sound of a shriek above me pulled me out of my morose thoughts, and I looked up to see one of my wing members dropping towards me before flying across town. I recognized who it was. They weren't on patrol today. They were just out for a flight.

I held back a smile and made my way back to my house, knowing I had other things to do. I needed to focus on my wing, my family, and the town.

My phone buzzed. I pulled it out of my pocket, answering without checking the readout.

"This is Jaxton."

"It's Rome," my best friend grumbled.

"What's up?"

"One of the guest wolf shifters took a nap, and her three teenage wolf pups decided to go on a rampage down Main Street."

I nearly tripped over my feet, imagining three teenage pups in wolf form, running through the middle of town, trying to burn down Ravenwood. I went on alert, scenarios of how this could be connected to Oriel and the necromancers filling my brain.

"Did they destroy anything?"

"Sorry, *rampage* is a little strong. I should have just

said shenanigans. They were in their human forms but are still learning their newfound strength since one of them may become alpha. At least that's what the wolf mom thinks. They accidentally broke a window while closing a door and did a few other things just being teenagers. They're doing their best to clean up the mess, and they're going to pay for it, but they could use your help learning how to fix a window."

I cursed, relief running through me. "Be better at the words you use, man."

"Sorry, it's been one of those days as a cleaner. I'm stuck at the den dealing with a couple of my elders. Do you have time?"

"I do. I'll work on this. Then I need to head down to my aerie."

"Sounds like a plan."

"I'm on it," I said and made my way to Main Street.

People were milling about, those in the know of the supernatural nodding at me and gesturing towards where the three teenagers stood. The humans who had no idea what surrounded them didn't even bother glancing past the broken glass or the bear in animal form walking past them.

With Sage's addition to the wards, it seemed that even that magic could hide in plain sight now.

I smiled at the thought, then looked at the bear shifter, who just shrugged. It seemed that Rome was testing the boundaries, or this bear shifter would have hidden a bit more than they were. It was good to know what we could and couldn't do. The next time the shifter leaders got together, we'd have to go over what Rome had found.

I shook my head and made my way towards the three teenagers.

"How are things going here?" I asked, donning my wing leader voice.

The kids stared at me and blinked.

"Oh, hi," the youngest said before ducking his head. The oldest nudged him, then met my gaze for a minute before lowering his head again. It seems that this one could have the scent of an alpha. They weren't going to challenge me or anything, and that was nice, but they definitely had that strength.

"Everything okay?" I asked.

The dominant one nodded. "We're very sorry. We didn't mean to break anything."

"Sometimes, we don't know our own strength," the middle one added, his gaze still lowered.

"It's okay. It happens. Were you giving your mama a break then?"

All three ducked their heads, blushing a bit.

"We're triplets. It's a little difficult sometimes."

They had to be fraternal ones since they didn't look alike, but much like the triplets that ran in the bear families, multiples weren't rare.

They weren't unusual within our wing, either, but it

had been a couple of years since a set was born. The last had been a set of quads nearly five years ago.

"We're really sorry," one of the guys said, and I nodded.

"I know you are. Now let me show you how to clean this up without magic, and then one of the witches will be by to make sure we do a good job."

"We like the town," the youngest said.

I smiled. This one had to be an omega. The way that they oozed emotion and wanted to soothe anyone around them. I already liked them. I wasn't sure about the middle kid, I liked him, but I didn't know what power he would hold. But he had some.

No wonder Mama Wolf had needed a nap.

"Okay, let's get to it. And I like this town, too. We take care of one another."

"We were only passing through, but Mom likes it. We're looking for a pack."

I froze as the two other teens looked down at the littlest one and frowned. I cleared my throat. "We don't have a wolf pack here. We do have bears, though."

"That's what Mom said. But when we had to leave our other pack, we came here, just to rest. But we're searching."

"Daymond," the eldest grumbled.

"No, it's okay. Does Rome know why you're here?" I asked cautiously. "The alpha of the bears?"

The one with the scent of the alpha nodded. "Yes. As

do the few wolves here. They said they were going to talk to Jaxton. That's you, right? The alpha, no...wait, the wing leader of the hawks."

"It seems I was out of commission for a time when they were going to talk to me. But, yes, that's me. Jaxton."

"Oh, hi," the one who could be an omega said with a smile. "Nice to meet you."

The other wolf cleared his throat. "Anyway, we just need some help cleaning up, I guess."

There was a story here. One I probably wouldn't like. But as I looked down at my phone, I realized I *had* missed a couple of calls when I was with Laurel. It seemed these wolves were on the run from something. I didn't know what it was, but hopefully, they'd be able to figure it out. With the strength of the eldest wolf, even if they were triplets, things could get interesting.

I helped the kids figure out how to clean up what they had messed up as well as fix the window when Rowen came by. She smiled and snapped her fingers. With a minor spell, she cleaned up any residual magic. She fluttered her fingers as she waved goodbye, and the three teenage wolves stared after her with their mouths agape.

I held back a snort and introduced myself to Mama Wolf as she came forward. I immediately knew that this submissive wolf had her hands full.

She was a strong wolf in terms of courage, but very submissive with three decently dominant boys and no other pack.

Rome and the others would help how they could. My job was to ensure that peace remained settled.

Before I could do any of that, I had to focus on my wing.

I nodded at the others, helped a few more people, and then finally made my way back home.

My people needed me. Eventually, I'd find time to think for myself. To just be.

But that wouldn't happen anytime soon.

I thought about shifting but decided I needed the walk. I'd take flight later, feel the wind beneath my feathers and my wings—despite the fact that I hated that song.

My lips quirked into a smile even if I didn't have much to smile about these days. Suddenly, I froze, a familiar scent on the wind.

"William?"

That was my cousin's scent, but that couldn't be right.

He was gone. Wasn't he?

I turned and ducked, flames erupting over my head.

"Tut tut tut. All alone, little hawk? What will you do when your feathers burn?" the necromancer in front of me whispered as she grinned.

My cousin, the man I'd thought dead, or at least long gone, stood behind her. He had his hand on her hip, and I sensed the mating bond. My heart raced at the implications of what I saw.

"William?" I asked as I rose, ducking another swath of flame.

"Cousin of mine, you don't want to mess with my mate, Renee. She's stronger than you. Stronger than the whole wing."

"What the hell?" I asked, trying to catch up to what was happening.

Was William mated to the necromancer? That meant he'd left the wing of his own volition.

There wasn't more time to think. Renee sent flame after flame, her control decent—what Laurel should have been—but the manic glee in her eyes scared me.

This was a witch, a necromancer, and revenants could be around any minute. As William came at me, slashing his talons towards me, I knew I was outnumbered. And I couldn't call for help.

And then Renee whispered a spell, something I couldn't quite hear, and flames danced along my flesh. My skin burned, my bones screamed, and then there was nothing.

Just talons across my stomach like knives digging into me, and the scent of burnt flesh filling my nostrils.

Laurel

"I don't see why we can't simply try," Ash said, his voice devoid of emotion as usual.

I pinched the bridge of my nose, breathing in deeply before slowly letting out the air.

I loved my brother, I cherished him, I respected him, and I liked him.

But ever since the curse had taken over, it was like he became a different person. Parts of him would always remain the same, but others continued to change.

He didn't quite understand the consequences of some of his actions. It wasn't that he wanted to put others in harm's way. It was more that he didn't realize that he was doing it until it was too late.

Or perhaps he didn't care. I wasn't sure how his curse

worked because he didn't tell me. Not that I told him about everything of mine, so I didn't know if I could truly blame him in that respect.

"Ash, I love you, but no, we can't try that."

"They're already dead. It's not like we could hurt them."

"We are not taking a revenant and seeing how to reverse the magic to stop it on a grander scale. If you talk with Rowen about the idea, she may curse you again to spite you."

"I think spiting and smiting and cursing could all be similar things," he added dryly, and I flipped him off.

"You're such a jerk."

"I'm your big brother. You love me."

I snorted. "Sure, whatever you say."

"As for the revenants, I'm not saying we experiment on them, but none of us knows much about necromancy because it's forbidden. We should try *something*."

"You know that you are one step closer to becoming dark once you even begin to think about that, and you have to be strong. More than any of us, you need to be strong, Ash."

He looked at me then, and I almost saw a glimpse of the brother I loved.

The one who used to smile with me and teach me magic alongside our parents. The brother who had laughed and always had a kind word or a joke for others.

The man who had fallen in love with Rowen and

made my best friend look lighter and happier than she ever had been.

Only that Rowen was gone. As was he.

"Did you ever find it weird that Mom and Dad named me Ash when you're the one with the fire?" he asked softly.

I blinked, once again wondering if this was my brother or if it was just who I missed. "Yes, but I thought they were just being ironic. After all, Mom said that there was seer blood in our family."

"Perhaps. Or perhaps she thought I would be the one with the flame."

"Maybe. But you have earth. You're part of this, Ash. Even if you leave."

"I don't think I'm leaving again, Laurel. I think this is it for me."

The way he said that didn't sound like he meant he was staying for good. Only that he would never leave.

Those were two far different ideas.

"We're not going to do that, Ash. Do you understand me?"

"I do, even if it makes it a little difficult to stomach. We're going in blind when it comes to Oriel and what he wants."

"He wants Ravenwood. He wants the power the coven holds, even if it is small. It has history and worth, and roots deeply embedded in the town. If Oriel comes for Ravenwood, he'll want all the magic that centuries-worth of Princes and Ravenwoods and Christophers have put into it."

"And what happens when he takes it?"

"We all perish," I whispered. "I need to go through a few boxes of inventory. Did you want to stay for a bit?"

Ash shrugged and then rolled up his sleeves and went to work. My brother was a billionaire. He excelled in real estate and finance and worked his ass off. He didn't steal. He didn't cheat. He didn't use his magic. He was just good with money and didn't need loopholes to make things happen.

He also tasked me with making sure that I found ways to use that money that wasn't evil.

With that said, my brother wasn't technically a billionaire anymore. He gave away enough that he had lost that status. And it was my job to ensure that happened.

Ash had an entire team to handle that for him, a company that didn't understand why he needed to give away so much of what he made. But then again, some part of him knew he needed to retain that aspect of himself.

And it was my job to ensure that.

That and working at Aunt Penelope's bookstore. Though, now I owned it. Only sometimes, it felt as if it were all futile, especially considering everything could burn up or blow up at any minute if the revenants came.

How many times had we fixed windows and

restocked and replaced floors and drywall because of magical attacks, accidental shifting, or the revenants?

Too many.

It sometimes felt like that was all we did—patching holes for the next attack, the next ending.

Ash worked in the back, his headphones in as he talked with his assistant and staff about a few work things. I let him be and worked on stocking the front area. We were closed for now because it was so late in the day—we kept different hours than we would if we were a nonmagical town.

The place was doing okay, and I didn't think I would go out of business anytime soon, but it still felt as if I were marking time and saving Penelope's place even though she would never be back.

I loved books—the way they felt, the way they smelled. I loved eBooks too. And audio. I just loved read-ing. Loved feeling like I could throw myself into any story or world and pretend that mine wasn't as bad as it was. I lived in a world of magic and the unknown, but it was books that genuinely brought me to that place. And that was why I liked romance more than anything. Because no matter where you went, no matter what path they took you down, no matter what pain was shoved in your face, you always knew what would happen. That was at least one aspect of the story. That the love you cherished, hoped for, and begged for would occur. There would be that happily ever after, even as the embers burned around you.

That didn't happen in real life. And as my power fluctuated within me, singeing my skin, I knew that it wouldn't happen for me.

But it was still nice to pretend.

At least, for the moment.

Someone banged on the door, and it shot open. I twisted, fire on my fingertips. My magic pulsated as I reached for my sword, only remembering that I had left it back with Ash.

"You!" Aiden, the wing's second, called before coming at me, moving faster than I'd ever seen him move. He had one hand around my throat in an instant, the other pinning me to the wall as he leaned forward. "Where is he?"

"What the fuck?" I gasped.

"Where is he?"

I pushed at him, trying to get him away from me, but there was a reason that Aiden was the second. I couldn't get out of his hold.

"Where is who?" I asked, coughing as he squeezed my neck even tighter. I couldn't breathe, and I scratched at him, trying to get away. But I would hurt him and anyone else in the vicinity if I used my magic. I needed my sword. I needed the one thing I *could* control.

"Laurel."

It wasn't a scream or a shout. It wasn't a growl.

But it was Ash.

He shoved out his hand and muttered a spell under his breath as he tossed Aiden away, the hawk rolling to the floor hard as I slid down the wall, rubbing my throat as I sucked in gulps of air.

My brother tossed me my sword. I caught it, grateful that he hadn't thrown it at my face.

Some days, it felt as if my brother wasn't entirely human. Occasionally, I was afraid he forgot what I was capable of.

"Are you declaring war on the coven then?" Ash asked, tilting his head as he studied Aiden. "Because you will be out of your league, little hawk. You're not even the strongest among your kind, and you think to come here and hurt my sister? You dare to hurt a witch?"

"You may be all-powerful, Christophers, but our wing can take you down. And we will if you don't tell us where our leader is."

I froze, ice chilling me even as it doused the flames. "Wait, where is Jaxton?" I asked as I scrambled to my feet, sword in hand.

Ash tilted his head, studying Aiden. "Why did you attack my sister if you lost your alpha?"

"Wing leader," Aiden spat. "And you know that. Stop trying to rile me. You were the last one Jaxton was seen with. Where the fuck is he?"

I swallowed hard, my hands shaking. "Why would you think I have him? Where did he go?"

"That's what we're asking *you*. You're lucky I'm the one who came. The elders want to gut you where you stand."

I had known the wing didn't like me. They had never liked me. They wanted their precious wing leader to mate with a nice little hawk, have nice little hawk babies, and stay within their nice little wing.

But that's not how the world worked. I would never be good enough for them. And now they thought I would hurt him? That I would kill him? Betrayal slashed at me, and I swallowed hard, pretending that I was fine. That I hadn't just felt betrayal wrapping its fingers around my neck and squeezing.

After all, Aiden had just done the same. I could still feel the pressure of his hands around my throat.

"Where is he?" I asked, flames dancing down my sword.

Ash cursed under his breath. "Stop using your magic."

I ignored him. "Why did you think I had anything to do with this?"

Aiden's eyes were bleak as he answered. "Because you were the last to see him. I told you that."

"We are in the middle of a cursed town with necromancers and revenants coming for us, and somehow it's me? Why would you think I would dare?"

Aiden's shoulders dropped, and it looked as if he were fighting himself. "The elders tasked me with questioning you. They used the power of the wing itself to force me.

I'm sorry." He let out a shaky breath. "Laurel, please help us find him."

I heard it then, the fear. Because those who surrounded him thought it was me, but he was the one tasked to find out. He could have killed me in an instant, snapped my neck, or taken me back to the clutch as if I had been the one who had hurt Jaxton.

Nobody would have been able to find me because Aiden was that strong. It appeared he was as conflicted as I was.

"Nobody's seen him since he left my house?" I ignored the way Ash glared at me and the fact that people had known Jaxton was at my house. There was no hiding that. There never had been.

Jaxton was mine, just as much as I wasn't his.

In that twisted way of my brain, at least.

"We don't know where he is, only that we scented blood. And then there was no trail. But we know it was magic. Magic took him away from us."

Fear clutched at my belly, and I glared at Aiden. "It could have been a necromancer. You do know that, right? I would never hurt Jaxton."

A pained look crossed the hawk's face. "We both know that's not true, even if you didn't mean to. We know that's not true."

Ash moved forward, and I stopped him, glaring at my brother.

"Ash."

"You're just going to let him talk to you like that?"

"I'm going to find out where Jaxton is."

Ash shook his head. "We can do a spell. Or I can."

"I know we can. So, we will."

"I am not letting you do a spell, little sister."

"I dare you to try to stop me," I glared and then I held up my hands, closed my eyes, and whispered under my breath.

"*Flame of fire, beam of light, bring me the gift of second sight. Find what I seek, show it to me, bless me now to clearly see.*"

Flames slammed into me, and my hands shook, bile filling my throat. I felt a trickle of blood coming out of my nose, and I ignored it. I had to.

My brother needed me to be stronger than this. Jaxton needed me to be stronger than this. I pushed away all thoughts of the pain and what it could mean and *searched*.

"What the hell do you think you're doing?" Rowen asked as she walked in, and I fell to my knees, the spell still working. I looked up at my best friend and Sage in the doorway, air and water flowing all around them.

"I need to find him." The desperation in my voice sounded as if I were being dragged over glass, but I couldn't hold back.

"That's all well and good, but you don't use a damn spell like that without us, and you sure as hell don't use it on your own."

Rowen stomped towards me, glared at Ash, and then knelt in front of me.

"I always knew you were a damn idiot. I didn't realize you had a death wish, as well."

"Stop it," Sage whispered between us. "Tell us what's going on and let us help." Sage knelt in front of me and gently wiped the blood from my face. "You know you shouldn't do spells like that alone."

"She's helping us find Jaxton," Aiden replied from my side, and both my brother and Rowen gave the hawk nearly identical glares.

It would have been funny if the memories of what wasn't weren't so painful.

"Excuse me? Who do you think you are right now? I see the bruises around her throat, and while Ash is many things, he wouldn't do that to his sister. I take it you're the one who hurt my coven sister?" Rowen asked, air billowing as it slammed Aiden into the wall. A few books fell, and I sighed.

"Let's not destroy the entire bookstore, shall we?" My body hurt, my soul ached, and I knew my attempt at humor fell flat.

"Speak, little hawk," Rowen growled. I had to hold back a smile. Rowen sounded so much like Rome just then. She never used her powers to hurt. But, apparently, Aiden had crossed a line.

The hawk lowered his head as if acknowledging exactly who the dominant one was in the room.

And it wasn't any of us.

Aiden shook his head. "The elder said it was her. That I was to get information out of her, no matter what."

"The elders are idiots," I growled. "You know that just as much as I do."

"Those are my people. Watch what you say." There wasn't much heat in his tone.

"And that is my sister you tried to kill," Ash spat.

Aiden narrowed his gaze. "I wasn't going to kill her."

"She was gasping for breath, so we're going to have to agree to disagree," my brother snapped.

"Enough," I said, the spell still pulsating within me. "I can feel it."

"Oh, you can feel it? Meaning you're close to figuring out what is happening right now? And where he is? You can do that on your own?" Rowen narrowed her eyes as she spoke, the painful sarcasm slicing.

"Rowen, just help."

"What do you think I'm trying to do, little one?"

She rarely called me that. When she leaned down and gripped my chin with her fingers, and Sage held my hand, magic suffused me, and I could breathe again. Whatever things had hurt before didn't as much now, and I could breathe.

"I can feel him."

"Okay, then, follow the path. We'll infuse you with what we can. But never do this again, do you understand me? Never do this again."

I nodded, knowing she was right. Realizing that I could have killed myself trying to find Jaxton. I was doing my best not to think about that, not to think about where Jaxton could be.

"You're saying he just disappeared? Without a trace?"

"There was blood, signs of an attack, but all we could scent was magic and fire."

My blood chilled, and Ash moved forward, his hands outstretched. Rowen stepped in front of him as if blocking him from hurting the hawk. I didn't blame her since we didn't want that situation on our hands, but it was definitely a close thing.

Rowen lifted her head. "Fire, as in the same magic the necromancer holds?"

"We weren't aware that the necromancer had fire. Jaxton isn't telling us much these days."

"But Nelle was there. Did you listen to Nelle? No," I spat. "Because your precious little elders never listen to anyone but another hawk. And even then, it's only a hawk they agree with."

He held up his hands and tried to say something, but I held up mine to stop him. "No, we're not doing this. Not now. We'll discuss how your precious little elders constantly disappoint you later."

"You don't know what you're talking about," he whispered.

"I know far too much." I rubbed my chest. "He's close."

"Good, then we'll find him."

"Find my brother?" Nelle said from the doorway, and I cursed again. Today was a day for everything, it seemed.

Aspen, the fae king with his mysterious eyes and practically glowing skin, stood beside the mermaid, his hand around her waist. I swallowed the urge to say something. Because, damn, that was interesting, wasn't it?

"We'll find your brother," Rowen promised.

Nelle raised her pointed chin. "You'd better, or you'll have to deal with me."

"You'll have to deal with all of *us,*" I whispered. "He's alive." The spell shook through me. "But I don't know for how long."

Ash met my gaze. "Then we'll find him. Together."

I stood, my magic draining me as more blood poured out of my nose and down my face. My coven stood around me, and I had to hope that my mate was still alive. That this wasn't the end.

That I wasn't going to lose everything before I even had a chance to claim it at all.

Laurel

My pulse pounded in my temples, but I ignored it, ignored the pain, and focused on what I could do. We needed to find Jaxton, and the only way that would happen before I passed out was if we worked as a team.

"I scent blood," Rome grumbled from beside me. I swallowed hard and turned to where the big bear shifter pointed.

"Is it Jaxton's?" I asked, my voice low.

Nelle and Aspen moved forward, the fae leader kneeling next to Rome as he nodded tightly. "It's him. However, it's not of death."

Nelle let out a small whimper, and then Aspen stood and held her close.

"This way," I whispered, my energy draining out of me.

Sage and Rowen stood on either side of me, their hands on my shoulders as they siphoned some of the spells from me. I was an idiot for not waiting for them, but all I could think about was finding Jaxton the only way I could.

I should have used a shifter to find him. Instead, I had used a spell, knowing it could be my last. But I hadn't cared, not when it came to him.

"He'll be here soon. I can feel him. But it also feels like something's trying to block me."

"I don't sense the necromancer close, but they were here." Rowen let out a breath. "I don't know how they keep getting through the wards, especially with as much as we're trying to strengthen them. That worries me."

"We'll figure it out." I turned to my brother as Ash did his best not to stare at Rowen. They were good at doing their best not to be in each other's orbits. And yet, that was all they did, constantly entered each other's spaces.

It seemed like the entire town was out searching for Jaxton or keeping the wards and Ravenwood safe. But if they weren't searching for the wing leader, they were circling the town, their dens, the aerie, or keeping people safe even if the humans and mundanes didn't know what was happening around them.

Jaxton was strong, fast, and brilliant. Nobody could get the drop on him, and yet they had. Somehow, they had. Now, we needed to find out how.

"Over here," I called and nearly fell to my knees as we turned the corner, and I looked under a fallen tree, one that had been charred. I nearly screamed. "Jaxton!" I leaned forward and put my hands on his face, doing my best not to cry.

Rowen barked out orders. "Rome, Ash, Aspen, work on the tree. We will work on Jaxton."

"I'll make sure the wing knows he's here," Nelle said as she bit her lip and turned to get one of the other hawks.

"If you're going to do a spell, don't you think you need me?" Ash asked, and I looked up at my brother when Rowen shook her head.

"Earth isn't needed in this spell. Otherwise, I would. I promise. For Jaxton, I would," she repeated, and my heart broke a little more for them. But I ignored it because Jaxton was hurt. He was so cold and he wasn't moving, but he *was* breathing. I had to remind myself that that was enough. For now.

"On three," Rome grumbled, and Ash moved to help the fae leader and alpha of the bears.

I heard a groan, wood splintering, and then caught the scent of smoke on the air as other hawks moved forward, circling us as the three men dragged the large tree.

Rowen took one hand, and Sage took the other.

Suddenly, I found myself in a circle around Jaxton's prone form.

Our coven leader raised her chin. "We'll do the spell."

"That is our wing leader. You will not touch him," one of the elder hawks snapped from beside me.

I turned to them, my flames blazing in my eyes even as pain and agony ripped through me. "We *will* save him, and you *will* step back. Your healer cannot fix this. A necromancer did it."

He spat at my feet, and I glared. "A witch did it. Now a witch is going to fix it? No, that's not how this works."

"You will cease, and you will let them heal him. You know who Laurel is to him," Aiden whispered.

My heart clenched at that, the twinge aching through me.

"She'll never be good enough for him," the elder outright said. I ignored the verbal slap and glared at Ash, warning my brother not to do something stupid like rip off a certain hawk's head. He could do it, and he *would* for me. However, we were trying not to be thorns in their sides. Murdering them probably wasn't the best idea.

"Laurel, with me," Rowen began, and I let out a breath, closing my eyes and focusing on the words I needed to say and my mate at my feet.

"*With this spell of beaming light, we mend what's hurt and make it right. Send energy through to cleanse and heal, our intentions set, manifestation real. Make Jaxton whole, we do decree. This is our will, so mote it be!*"

I opened my eyes as Jaxton's body bucked, and I let out a sharp breath, annoyed with myself for letting my emotions get the better of me. More blood dripped from my nose, but I let it fall, knowing that blood magic also had a purpose.

"Laurel, it's not enough."

Jaxton hadn't woken, and my heart broke with each passing moment. I didn't need Rowen's words to understand that.

"There's another spell you can do," Ash said from my side as he knelt beside us and looked down at Jaxton in my arms.

"She's not strong enough." There was no censure in Rowen's words, only fear.

I glared at my friend.

"Whatever you think I need to do," I said, my hands shaking, "I'll find a way to be strong enough."

Ash let out a breath and held out his hands, sliding a knife into his palm. I hadn't even realized he had a blade on him. The shifters and the fae around us each let out a sharp growl or moans.

"Warn us before you start bleeding," Rome whispered.

"You know what to do."

I nodded and held up my palm. As Ash sliced it, I ignored the pain. I was already aching so badly that my mind barely registered the cut. Rome continued growling, looking as if he wanted to save Sage from all of this. I shook my head and then joined hands with my brother.

"It's Christopher blood. I won't hurt your mate."

Rowen started to mutter under her breath, but I didn't focus on her. Instead, I focused on who I needed and began to chant.

"*On this day and in this hour, we call upon the Christopher power. Earth and fire we do combine, to bring back he who is mine. In this moment, our lives our bound, turning life from lost to found. Return to me as you should be, this is my will, so mote it be!*"

Tears slid down my cheeks as agony ripped its claws over my body, flames searing me beneath my flesh. My soul burned, the flames encroaching on my very essence. And yet it wasn't enough. It would never be enough.

I looked down and let out a sob. "Jaxton." I leaned down and pressed my lips to his as he smiled.

"I knew you'd find me," he rasped.

"Wing leader," the elder whispered as he knelt beside me. "Who did this?"

"We all know who did it, Elijah," Rowen snapped. "Give him some space. Give them both space."

"You are not of our wing. You do not understand."

I looked at the other man, my flames wanting to reach out. But I knew that this wasn't the time or the place for that—nor did I have the energy, not after three spells back-to-back.

"You will give me space with my mate. You know what spell I just did and how I need him near me. You may be his wing, but I am his, as well. You shouldn't forget that." He knew the cost of what had been taken just now.

Elijah sneered. "You have no mating bond. You have no authority over the wing. You should remember that, girl, before you kill him along with everyone else you're sending to hell."

"That's enough. If you do not want to deal with an incident that crosses all town boundaries, you will give him space."

I looked up at Aspen, wondering why he was standing up for me. Then I thought about it. Aspen and Nelle were growing close. And considering that Nelle had her issues with the wing, not her brother, it made sense that everything seemed as if it were too much right then.

"I'm fine, Elijah," Jaxton said as he shook his head and leaned up. I sat next to him and held him close, even as he glared at the others around us. "We have a lot to discuss."

"What did you see?" Elijah asked, and I let out another snarl.

"Seriously? He just said he needed time."

Jaxton squeezed my hand and then stood, pulling me with him. With the spells we had used on him, he would be back to normal within the hour. I was the one weakened and needing aid. I leaned against him, hating that anyone saw me weak, but there was no holding back at the moment.

"Renee came after me."

"Renee? That's the necromancer's name?" Rowen asked as she moved forward.

"Yes. Renee. She's a fire witch, a necromancer, and a higher-order one from what I could tell."

I cursed under my breath. "Meaning she can bring back shades. Not just the revenants."

"That's all your area of expertise. But from what I could tell, she's stronger than Faith was."

"That means Oriel is not the necromancer with fire. At least as far as we know."

"No, not that we can tell."

"She just came at you?"

Jaxton looked around as the pulse in my temple began to beat hard again. "I was walking home after I helped those three wolves," he began. At my look of confusion, he explained about the three teenagers without a pack, and Rome nodded as if everyone understood what was going on. I didn't. However, I wasn't a shifter. I was barely a witch. And we didn't have time for me to keep asking questions.

"So, I wasn't the last person you saw before it happened?" I asked, glaring at Aiden and the others.

"Why would you think that?" Jaxton asked before blinking and looking at the bruises on my neck. "Who. Hurt. You?" he gritted out, one word at a time.

"I'm fine, Jaxton. I took care of it."

"I helped," Ash added.

Jaxton turned and glared at his wing. "You hurt her?

You thought she did something to me? Laurel. Of all people. You thought she did something to me?"

"You're not in your right mind when you're around her, wing leader," Elijah whispered.

"We'll speak about this later. I don't have time for how you're reacting right now or the way you're treating my mate."

I ignored how it made me feel when he called me his mate, especially considering that I had called him much the same. We seemed to be skipping steps, as if we were claiming one another, knowing there wouldn't be a happy ending. Because with those spells, I knew I didn't have much energy left.

Jaxton wouldn't be able to save me, but we could call each other mates as if any of that made sense.

"She found you. That's all that matters," Aiden whispered.

"No, I don't think it does. But we will discuss it. However, she's not the one who betrayed us. She's not the one who attacked me. You know who was?" He paused, his shoulders shaking. "It was our cousin," he whispered as Nelle sucked in a breath.

I blinked. "Your cousin?"

"William. The one we thought was dead. He seems to be mated to Renee, the dark fire witch. And he was here. He was the one who did this." Jaxton lifted his shredded shirt, and I let out a curse, holding my hand above his newly healed flesh.

"I thought it was just burns."

He shook his head as he looked at me. "No, talon slices, as well. Your spell, whatever you did—and we will talk about you using magic later—" he added, "seems not to have healed it all."

"You see? Our healer could have helped him," Elijah spat. This time, Rowen was the one to whirl on him. "Enough, old man. You might think you're helping, but all you're doing is creating tension within our ranks. Who is this William?" she asked for all of us.

"He's our cousin. He left the wing over a year ago now, and we all thought he was dead." Jaxton rubbed his heart with his fist. "The bond broke, and he was just...gone. We all thought he died. But he didn't."

"Are you sure you weren't seeing things because of some witch magic crap?" Elijah asked. This time it was Aiden who stopped Elijah. Not with a word, but with a fist. Elijah went down, and I winced as the elder let out a gust of air. However, with the way he acted and given that we were not human, I didn't blame anyone in this situation.

"I don't know what they want, but they needed me down. They didn't tell me why. They just attacked. And with whatever magic she has, and how William is nearly as strong as me? I couldn't stop it."

I reached out and cupped Jaxton's face. "You survived."

"Just. But you found me, and we're outside town limits."

I hadn't even noticed. But given the way Rowen's whole body looked as if it were strained, I knew she had.

"Can you be outside of the town wards for long?"

My sister witch shook her head. "No, I need to get back soon. With the way we're fluctuating in power and energy, it's good for me to be close. I can stay away, but not if we're using this much magic."

What she was saying wasn't a secret, but I knew she hated revealing her weaknesses.

"Come, then. I'll make sure you get back," Ash insisted.

Rowen raised her chin. "I'm fine. I know the way."

"You shouldn't go alone," Sage put in. "It's safer to be in pairs. Especially with everything that just happened."

"Because we still don't know what's going on," I added. "We don't know what they want other than our town and our power. If they get in and get us, if they find the nexus of our town's energy, who knows what they'll do. And it's not only the witches," I added for the shifters' benefit. "It's how our town blood and energy thrives on the fae and the shifters and the mermaids and all the connections we have. Without the town, we'd die. Without us protecting the town, anyone who came in could use the energy for their own greed."

"If we're not careful, we'll lose more than the town.

More than the people in it. We'll lose our very soul and existence."

I swallowed hard at Jaxton's words, even if what he said was true. "We have to stop them. No matter the cost."

Jaxton leaned down and kissed me as if nobody were watching, though many people were. "We'll protect this town and *you*. Because that's a price I'm not willing to pay."

Elijah grumbled under his breath, but I ignored the older man. I had nearly killed myself protecting Jaxton, and I knew he would do the same for me.

"We have a checklist," Rome grumbled. "Find William, find Renee, find Oriel. Figure out how to break the curses, figure out how to protect the town, and plan a wedding. We've got it."

I looked at him and blinked at the last part. "Really? You're just going to conflate a wedding like that?"

"We need happiness, and weddings can be happy. And not at all stressful. And if I have to pretend that that's what I'm planning instead of having to deal with magic and shifters and everything completely unknown to me a year ago? That's what I'll deal with."

I looked at them, at Jaxton, then at the retreating backs of Ash and Rowen, both of whom had left without a word because I knew Rowen needed to be within the town borders quickly. And I knew that we didn't have much time.

We might think we knew what Renee's motivation was, but she had done something. She had made a mistake.

She had dared to hurt my mate, and now, as soon as I found her, I'd make her pay. Even if it killed me.

Which, given how the magic pulsated within me, wasn't far off, despite any spells my coven might want to find and try for me.

CHAPTER
TWELVE

Jaxton

Though it wasn't a mating bond between us, I still felt something pulsating between Laurel and me. I wasn't sure what it was, but it was something. They had said that the spells she had used connected us in some way, and I guessed they were right. I just hadn't expected it to be like that.

I could sense her. Feel her.

I knew that if she left, it would feel like someone were ripping my heart out. Was that what a mating bond felt like? I wasn't sure I even wanted to know.

"You should be sitting down," Laurel declared from

beside me, and I looked over at her from the front of the bookshop.

I blinked and shook my head. "You're the one who should be sitting down. You used your energy to protect me. While I might be fine, you're in pain."

She shrugged. "I'll be okay. The coven helped."

"At the end, not at the beginning," Rowen snapped from beside us, and I blinked at the ferocity in her tone.

"I'm fine, both of you."

I wasn't sure I believed Laurel.

"If you were fine, we wouldn't constantly be cleaning blood off your face from your nosebleeds."

My gaze shot to hers, and I nearly growled. "How many nosebleeds have you had?"

"Enough," Rowen snapped again.

My mate raised her chin. "I needed to find you. Don't get on my case. I needed to find you. And so, I did."

"You did. Yet you could have died doing so. You have to stop doing things like that for others, Laurel. You should've asked for help or done something else. You didn't need to hurt yourself for me."

She narrowed her eyes at me. If looks could have killed, I'd be lying on the floor in a puddle. "I will do anything I have to, to ensure you are safe. You keep saying the same about me. So, here we are. Trying to protect one another. And that's what we'll do. Try to protect one another."

"I'm sorry," I whispered.

"I'm sorry, too."

Rowen looked between us and sighed. "Both of you should be resting. The healing spells and the other ones we used to find you, Jaxton, really should make you feel as if nothing happened, but it did. The necromancer and a hawk almost killed you."

"You don't have to remind me. I was there."

I had nearly died. I vividly remembered seeing my cousin's face as he smiled at me with a look I had never seen before and the way his talons had felt when they dug into my flesh.

"Laurel should be resting, though," I added.

"She should, but she's Laurel, so she's not going to."

"I'm standing right here. I'm going to help clean up the mess from the spells, and then I'm going to clean my sword. All while ensuring that Jaxton doesn't do too much."

"You just heard Rowen. I'm fine. You're the one who used too much magic for the spell."

"Rowen didn't say that. You're projecting."

"Well, if the two of you are going to continue fighting without telling each other how you feel, I'm just going to head over here and work at my shop. I'll be there if you need me."

Rowen moved forward, cupped my face, and kissed me gently on the mouth.

I grinned at her, shaking my head. "You are trouble," I whispered.

"I am glad that you are safe, brother mine. Remain that way and watch out for our girl."

Rowen gave Laurel a withering stare and then headed back to her spell shop.

Sage and Rome had already made their way to her place since somebody needed to run the bakery.

I didn't know how much longer the three of them would be able to keep their shops open with the revenant and necromancer attacks we were dealing with, but perhaps they could find a way. They were good at that.

"Are you okay?" I asked thoughtfully.

"I should be asking you that question."

"Then I'll answer. I'm fine. Whatever you did helped. I'll be forever grateful." I paused, wondering how to bring this up.

"This bond that I feel between us. Will it fade?"

Laurel met my gaze and swallowed hard. "It might. It probably will. It might not go away completely like it would with anyone else, though."

My hawk slashed me with its talons, and I reined it in.

"I hope you never feel this with anyone else."

Her lips quirked into a smile. "Possessive much?"

"With you? Always."

She sighed and shook her head. "We should get back to the bookstore. It's time to pretend that the world isn't ending."

I gripped her hand and pulled her closer. When I crushed my mouth to hers, she didn't resist. Instead, she leaned into me as if this were the most casual thing in the world.

"Laurel. We're going to beat this. All of this. You see what happens when we work together. We find answers."

"I wish that were the case. But it's hard to have faith when everything hurts."

I scowled and tugged her inside, forcing her to sit behind the desk.

"You get some work done, do something. I will work the front."

"Really? You don't have to be with your wing or something?"

"I should." Guilt slid into me, but I needed a moment to breathe, to think.

Because my people had tried to hurt her. They *had* hurt her. She still had bruises on her neck from Aiden. My second was very lucky that Laurel held me back from doing something about it.

The door opened, the little bell tinkling above it as Aspen and my sister walked through. The leather-clad mermaid and equally leather-clad fae king nodded at me, and I narrowed my eyes.

The two had been spending a lot of time together, but I had been holding back my curiosity and big-brother tendencies. It wasn't the fae king with all of his mysterious power that I worried about. No, it was my sister.

Mermaids could be vicious, especially when you weren't looking or ready for it.

"We just wanted to check on you." Nelle moved forward and let go of Aspen's hand to come and kiss me on the cheek. I wrapped my arms around her and hugged her close. She sank into my hold, my baby sister clinging to me. "I thought you were dead," she whispered.

"Honestly, I thought I was, too."

She let out a little noise, one that echoed Laurel's.

I looked over Nelle's head to see my mate coming forward, ignoring my order to sit down. Not that she ever listened to me when it came to orders.

"You're both resting and healing then?" Aspen asked as he studied us.

I narrowed my eyes at him, and he just smirked, not one of a man who wanted to die today, but one who thought he knew what I was thinking. I didn't blame him. It seemed he was seeing my younger sister, and I wanted to know why nobody was talking about it, even though it seemed everybody wanted to talk about it.

"Stop glaring at Aspen."

I looked down at Nelle. "Is there a reason I *shouldn't* be glaring at the man who dared to touch my baby sister?" I teased.

She shoved me, and a smile played on my lips as Laurel barked out a laugh. "Oh, good. Let's worry about you, Nelle, so he can stop puttering around me."

"I do not putter."

"I would say it's more of a hover," Aspen added deadpan.

I scowled at the other man. "Either you're on my side in this, or you're the one touching my baby sister. Make your choice."

"Really, Jaxton? That's the line you're going for? The broody big brother who has a weird fascination with who his sister dates?"

"I'd say '*a-ha you're dating him*,' but that point seems moot at this juncture."

"Of course, we're together," she said as she rolled her eyes.

Aspen let out a long sigh. "I didn't feel the need to ask for your permission, wing leader. But I can if that will help ease the tension between our peoples."

My lips felt the urge to smile, and Laurel laughed outright as she wrapped her arms around my waist and leaned into me. This felt...right. As if we should have been doing this long ago.

"You do not have to worry about me, Aspen."

"No, we only have to worry about the elders," Nelle grumbled.

"I will deal with them shortly," I said after a moment, my hawk gliding in aerials within me.

"You shouldn't have to. People should respect you and agree with you. They're not going to blame William on you, are they?" Nelle asked, her eyes wide.

I shook my head. "No, they won't blame me. Still, I

need to get there soon and deal with the ramifications. But I spent nearly two hours with them earlier today, trying to find some semblance of peace. But we're not like the bears. We don't come together in a ball and cuddle. We're loners. It's what we do."

Hawk shifters were different than any other shifter types. Maybe other birds of prey were the same, but we didn't know. We didn't keep in contact with them because we were different.

That was the whole point. We didn't cling to our wing when things got hard. We were insular, and my job was to find ways to connect us without forcing the bonds that would hinder our ability to soar and fly.

That was why the elders pushed so hard. Why, while I was the strongest, the leader, I still had to answer for certain things.

Sometimes, I thought it would be easier to be a bear. To be like Rome. And then I remembered the pain he had gone through with Alden. I figured maybe there wasn't an easy way to be a shifter or even to be a part of Ravenwood.

"Did me staying away help?" Laurel asked, and I cursed.

"Honestly, I was going to ask the same thing," Nelle said with a shrug. This time, Aspen cursed. He held her close like I did with Laurel, and the fae king and I gave each other a look.

Oh, there would be retribution. I just wasn't sure how we would go about it.

Aspen froze and tilted his head to the side, right as the hairs on the back of my neck stood on end.

"Revenants," Laurel called out as she pulled out her sword. "I'm getting tired of this Renee and her ability to raise the dead."

"You're not alone," Nelle said as she pulled out a dagger.

"I don't think so," Aspen said as he pushed her behind him. "You know you're not prepared yet."

"You've been training me."

"I thought I had been training you to fight," I muttered as my talons grew out of my fingertips.

My sister narrowed her gaze. "You both have been. And I'm going to fight. For my family, and for this town."

"You won't be alone," Rowen said from the doorway as she and Sage walked in. Ash and Rome were nowhere to be seen, but that was probably a good thing. They needed to be downtown while we were inside the small bookstore, dealing with whatever was coming.

Then, there was no more time to speak.

The first revenant smashed through the window, and Laurel let out a growl before she attacked. I was at her side, sliding my talons into the nearest revenant as she sliced off its head.

We did more of the same, working in tandem as if we'd been doing it all our lives.

Maybe we had, in a sense. I felt the bond within us, both of us moving as one in some respects. I didn't know if this was what it would be like once the mating bond finally took hold, but I wanted it.

I wanted what we couldn't have.

"We need the spell," Rowen called as she looked across the back alley. "More are coming. The forest is filled with them."

"Do you have enough energy for a spell?" I asked, worried.

Laurel looked at me and nodded. "If you hold my hand, I'll be okay because of the way we're connected."

Something sparked in the back of my mind. An answer. But it faded away as fast as it came.

"Quickly, do the banishment," Aspen said calmly as he moved forward. "I'll keep them off you as the four of you stay in your circle with the spell."

"And I'll be by your side," Nelle said as she tossed a dagger straight into a revenant's head. It slid between its eyes, the revenant falling. She ran forward, dug the dagger out, and continued tossing it.

She was a far better fighter than she had been even last month, and I had to credit Aspen with that since my head had been up my ass, dealing with Laurel.

"Come now, join hands."

We stood in a line, me at the end holding Laurel's hand. I would take whatever fire and pain she needed to get rid of, anything to save my mate.

"*Earth, air, water, fire, bring us that which we desire. Stop this evil, purge this blight, banish this death to darkest night. Lord and Lady, ancestors, too, lend us your strength for what we must do. Take this darkness so we may be free. This is our will, so mote it be!"*

Fire erupted down my arms. Even though I couldn't see it, I felt it. Laurel screamed and nearly fell to her knees before I caught her, bringing her close.

I grabbed her sword from her hand as she fell and slashed out at the closest revenant.

It opened its mouth as if to scream, but there was no sound.

And then the revenants were gone, the jarring sound of bodies hitting trees as they flew through them echoing within my brain.

I fell, the sword clattering at my side as Laurel climbed into my lap.

"That was stronger than before," Sage said as she staggered into Aspen. Aspen held Nelle's hands as he kept Sage up, and I looked at Rowen.

She looked stronger than she ever had, as if she were somehow able to breathe now, to not push so much of her soul and energy into the town.

She looked like a goddess.

Like a Ravenwood.

"I think we're finally becoming a coven."

As I looked down at Laurel, noticing how she curled into herself, I had to wonder at the cost. She had nearly killed herself to save me, therefore creating the temporary bond between us.

Would a mating bond fix that? Or would it end us both before we even had a chance to begin?

CHAPTER
THIRTEEN

Laurel

"I'm glad that we're doing this. We haven't had a lot of time with just each other these days. To just breathe."

I looked up at Sage as she spoke and smiled softly. "You're right."

"We've been focusing on defense, and matings, and curses, and the town, but not really on us. Maybe it's time we do our best to do that. And I'm just as guilty of not doing it, if not more so than the rest of you."

I shook my head at Rowen. "We're all equally guilty of ignoring part of our coven responsibilities. Or perhaps it's that we're trying to do it all. And if you want to talk about who has more responsibility in that, it could be me. Considering I have been hiding from exactly what we could be doing for how long now?"

"If you're done slapping at yourself for what you just told Rowen not to do, maybe we can continue our girl time?" Sage asked sweetly as she fluttered her eyelashes at me. I snorted and shook my head.

"All I'm saying is that it's nice to be here."

Rowen's home had been in her family for generations. It sat on the land of the original settlers and had been built soon after the original founding members' children decided to expand. Time had changed some of the structure, but the bones of the glorious home were still the same. I didn't live in the Christophers' original home. In fact, no one did as it had burned down in a cursed accident in my grandparents' time.

The Christophers carried the curse on their soul, and I knew until Ash and I each found a way to rid ourselves of our particular curses, any children that may be born down our line would also carry the curse. Not that I thought children were coming soon. Ash would never procreate, not with what lay heavy on his heart and in his body, and I couldn't. I wouldn't be around long enough for that. And I didn't think my body would survive a pregnancy anyway. What would the flame and fire power do to a fetus?

I shivered, and Rowen glanced at me, concern on her face. "What's wrong?"

"Thinking of something I'd rather not talk about."

"We're here for a girls' night. We should talk about everything. What's wrong?" Sage asked.

"Honestly? I was thinking about what would happen if I got pregnant. With the curse."

Rowen's mouth went into a thin line, and I knew it wasn't anger or censure but the fact that she couldn't help. She had been trying for our entire lives, and we hadn't been able to fix it. Rowen was the most powerful witch I knew. She had strength, beauty, grace, and sheer talent.

And yet, she couldn't fix this.

It wasn't just me or the town she was trying to free. Ash was the other side of my cursed coin, and she couldn't save him either.

I knew that it had to break her far more than anything that could happen to me, not that I would tell her that. Not that I would tell anybody that.

"I'm sorry," Sage whispered. "Not that me saying that actually helps."

I shrugged and played with the stem of my wine glass. We sat in Rowen's living room on the ornate yet comfortable chaise lounges and couches, and I wanted to take another sip of my drink but knew it would taste of ash and nothingness. Not because of the magic of the curse, but because I wasn't sure I wanted to taste anything just then.

"I know that we will fix this. The town will not end,

you will not have your curse, and you and Jaxton will have little baby hawk shifter-witches, and we will have happiness."

I looked at Sage and heard the desperation and determination in her voice. "That would be wonderful if it were true. But is it?"

"Do you think your children would have hawk shifter or witch DNA?" Sage asked, a small smile on her face.

We were going to pretend, and I was okay with that for now because I needed to pretend, too.

"Knowing Jaxton and his dominance, they'd probably all be little hawk shifters." I would honestly love that, but I couldn't let myself dream.

"Would the wing approve of that?" Rowen asked, tapping her fingers on the desk.

"All hypothetical, of course?"

"Of course," Rowen answered, knowing that this conversation was a little too much for me, but I knew where Rowen wanted it to go.

"I think the wing will have problems with anyone who isn't a pure hawk. They already have problems with Nelle and with how much time Jaxton spends with me. I'm not a fan of those elders, but there *are* good people in the wing, those who agree that mating outside of the wing is a good thing."

"Just like with the bears. If they didn't want to mingle with other magical creatures and humans, then why live in a magical town full of them?"

"Exactly," Rowen added. "As leaders of the witches here, even those with a small percentage of magical blood, we all know that blending the populations isn't an issue. It's the elders or those who want to try to scramble for any semblance of power who feel that way. And we all know what happened to Alden when he tried."

Sage's eyes narrowed. "We do. And just like with the bears, the hawks will realize what they're doing. Jaxton's a good person. As are a lot of his people. Nelle might think she's not fully welcomed, but they love her. She's so good with the baby hawks and hatchlings or whatever they're called," Sage added with a grimace. "I used to be so good at learning new things. Now, I feel like I'm playing catch-up with all these magical terms. There's only so much I can read in a book to understand exactly what I'm missing from not being in the magical world for over two decades."

"First, as a bookstore owner, you can find everything in a book."

"That might be true." Rowen smiled.

"Second, the babies are called hatchlings. And sometimes, even the teenagers, the fledglings, are called hatchlings when they act like babies. Nelle is included in many of the customs and routines with the wing, but not everything. She is, however, treasured within the mermaid community."

"Because her father is the king?" Rowen asked.

I shook my head. "They love her for her. However, her

brother is the wing leader, and her mother is the former wing leader's mate. You would think it would be the same case with the hawks, but the mermaids understand."

"They also have connections all over the world, rather than set in stone in their little aerie." Sage shrugged at my look. "I'm not saying it's perfect, or that they're perfect since I don't really know many of the mermaids beyond Nelle, but perhaps being connected to so much of the world helps."

"Perhaps." I sighed. "Either way, I'm not going to have children with Jaxton."

"You don't think you're truly mates?" Sage asked, her eyes filled with curiosity and hope.

I bit my lip and looked down at my hands. "No, we are," I whispered. "But if we create a bond beyond the small healing one that's already fading between us, I could burn him right alongside me when the curse finally takes me."

"We're not going to let that happen," Sage promised. "And when we break the curse, will you mate with him?"

Tears pricked the backs of my eyes, and I swallowed hard. "If I am able to break this curse and have a future in this town and in the world, I would mate with him in an instant. He's mine. He has always been, even if I didn't let myself think that."

Even saying the words settled a new weight on my shoulders. A purpose, or perhaps a promise.

I didn't know. And I was afraid to focus too much on it

because if I did, I would realize what I was missing once everything ended.

"Let's talk of things not so serious, like this duo who keeps attacking our town," Rowen said as she drained the last of her wine glass.

I snorted, did the same to my glass, and then got up to get the bottle of champagne out of the ice bucket on the table. I poured some for each of us and then plopped a cheese cube into my mouth. "I love Havarti," I mumbled around the cheese.

"I know. I made sure I had extra for you."

"Add smoked gouda and brie, and I think I'm dying in soft cheese heaven."

Rowen smiled though I still saw strain in her gaze. "I added a few harder kinds for all of us since those were good, too."

"Those are great with the smoked meats you have," Sage said as she danced in her chair, piling her little plate with food.

I smiled and did the same. I was constantly starving since my body burned more energy than the others. I ate like a shifter with how much food I had to consume to keep up with the curse and my fire power. I wasn't sure what would happen if we broke the curse. Maybe I could eat less. But as of now, I ate like a bear, and I still could barely keep up with it. If the flames stopped burning everything inside me, I might be able to eat a single hamburger in a sitting instead of four.

"I popped another cheese cube into my mouth, smiled at the smoked gouda, and then sighed as I remembered what Rowen had asked.

"William is Jaxton's cousin."

"And he betrayed the wing. If he's working with a necromancer, *mated* with her, his soul will be as dark and twisted as hers."

While I understood what Rowen was saying, I didn't want to believe that. Especially when we were discussing souls. My family had a touchy idea about how a soul could be changed, used, or lost.

"We don't even know where they're staying."

Rowen shook her head at Sage's words. "No, the shifters have been sending out trackers and scouts, the same with Aspen and his fae. And while I've done spells, something is blocking us. Perhaps Oriel."

"I want to know who the hell this Oriel is. Who he thinks he is. Because if he wants the magic at the core of the town, he'll have to get through us. And I realize that's exactly what he's doing, but we're stronger together."

I hadn't even realized I was going to say the words until Rowen's smile widened.

My coven sister leaned forward. "Hell, yes. He's not going to be able to take us down. But I'm afraid he'll hurt those weaker along the way. You already saw what he did with sneaking his people into town and letting his revenants creep in. He wanted Jaxton down for a reason...why?" She looked pointedly at me, and I swallowed hard, knowing where she was going.

"I don't know how Jaxton's supposed to be the one to help me through this curse. Maybe it's not that at all. Perhaps it's taking out a wing leader or killing him and breaking me so I can't function within the coven."

"It could be all of that," Sage said.

"Then what are we supposed to do? We can't find this Oriel. We can't find his people, and yet they're coming after us. Our coven is supposed to be the strongest there is, yet we can't do anything." I was afraid it was me—my power. Because my connection to Jaxton, however tentative, had given me more strength and stability to make the coven stronger. With her new powers, Sage could help as well, so it wasn't all on Rowen. All three of us had to be strong and determined to make the coven work as prophecy had always dictated.

Only I was the problem. And I knew it.

Before I could say anything on that, however, I sensed someone behind me and turned to see the men walking in.

The three were a unit as if they always had been, as they were when they were younger. All they were missing was Trace. I knew that even though it hurt to think about him not being here, I didn't break anymore when thinking about it.

Rome came in first, his eyes only for his mate. He leaned down, plucked her up from the chair, and kissed her hard on the mouth, something far deeper and more intimate than normally done in front of a group.

Jaxton came to me, and I sat up and looked at him, a smirk on my face as he looked over at Rome and Sage. He rolled his eyes, brushed my hair back from my face, and kissed me gently. "Hello there."

"Hi," I breathed, feeling like an idiot. I couldn't think when he was around, couldn't say anything.

We all pointedly didn't look over at Rowen as Ash sat on the couch opposite me, the spot closest to Rowen but not touching her.

Of course, he didn't touch her. He didn't even look at her. But we all knew that this was the core six. How it always should've been.

If the Christophers hadn't been cursed outside the town's curse, this should have led us into the next part of the prophecy to protect Ravenwood. But that wasn't the case.

Because my brother and I didn't have the future we should.

The curse that told us the town would one day fall to the darkness if the coven didn't strengthen was only part of our worries.

I looked at Ash and swore I saw a glimpse of the man he'd been. The pain of what we had lost flashed in his eyes but was gone again in an instant as if he couldn't feel anything.

This was not my brother. He had been growing colder,

and more dangerous with each passing month, and I was so afraid that even as we did our best to try to save him and me, we wouldn't be strong enough.

We were going to lose what we had or what we could have had. I would flame, and Ash would turn to ice, and we would break.

And then the town would fall.

It was hard to have hope. Even looking at Sage and Rome and how they had overcome all of their obstacles, it was hard.

I used my sword, gritted my teeth through the pain, and fought.

I didn't give up.

As I looked at Jaxton, saw the love in his eyes, felt feeling stirring within me, the yearning for that bond that could never be, I didn't want to give up.

And perhaps that was a vow I needed to make—one that I would break if fate had anything to say about it.

FOURTEEN

Jaxton

The following day, it felt as if our moment of bliss and relative calmness could end at any moment. I hovered over my mate and kissed her gently. She opened hazel eyes to me and smiled. I didn't see the flame behind the irises, didn't see the heat and the pain. For that one moment, she was mine. As I was hers. That she could have this moment of clarity and peace nearly brought me to my knees.

"Good morning," she whispered before shifting a bit and wincing. She must have tugged on the burn scars on her side. I leaned down to kiss her shoulder gently above the new burn. It would heal soon, her scars fading even as they increased in frequency and horror.

She was in an endless cycle of a curse I couldn't break, but she was still mine, and I would die to protect her, even if she wouldn't let me.

"What time is it?" she asked as she stretched her arms over her head. I groaned at the sight of her breasts pressing against me and leaned down to lap at her nipple. She moaned, sliding one hand through my hair as I sucked gently on the beaded tip.

"Early enough that I wanted to wake you my way."

Her legs spread, and I slid between her welcoming thighs before moving to her other nipple and gently biting down. She arched into me, her mouth parting as she ran her fingers down my sweat-slick back.

After we left Rowen's, all of us doing our best to formulate a plan for rotating shifts of protection and other spells we could do to find Oriel, we had come to my house rather than hers. I needed to be near my people and it had gone unspoken that we would spend the evening together.

We hadn't bonded yet, and I didn't know if she would let herself give in, but I wanted her to. I wanted her to trust our fate enough for that to happen.

Only with the pain in her eyes, even as I gently kissed and nibbled on her breasts, I wasn't sure fate would be that kind to us.

"Your eyes have gone all smoky and worried."

I blinked away the tension and then kissed her again on the lips before gently laying another trail of kisses down her body.

"Shh, I need to have my breakfast."

She moaned, letting out a soft laugh as I kissed down her belly and hips before settling myself between her open thighs.

"Already so wet for me."

"It seems to be a common occurrence when I'm around you. Even when we're supposed to be working and talking about dangerous things, my panties go damp, and all I want is you inside me."

I traced my fingers along her lower lips, gently probing her entrance. She let out a shocked gasp before lifting her hips slightly towards my face. "I guess I'll have to remedy that. Of course, thinking about you wet in front of me when there's nothing I can do about it means I'll be hard as a lead pipe until the end of my days."

"Oh, poor you. That thick dick all nice and hard for me. Whatever shall I do?"

I grinned before leaning down to gently press my mouth to her. She groaned, her hands moving to her breasts as she played with her nipples. The sight nearly sent me over the edge.

She was glorious, her brownish-red hair like a fiery halo on the pillow. The more she used her powers these days, the redder her hair got, and I loved it. She was all sensual woman, the anchor of her tattoo shifting around her body in sweet flames as my anchor flew around my back, enjoying the sensation of touching our mate.

I ate to my heart's content, licking and sucking and pleasuring every inch of her as I gently paid more attention to her clit.

Her breaths came in sharp pants as she neared the edge. When I spread her wider for my attentions, and gently blew cool air over her, she let out a shocked gasp. She was nearly there so I sucked on her again, inserted one finger into her pussy, my thumb gently probing her back entrance. She froze for an instant, but then I used her wetness to ease my thumb inside, loving the way she clamped around me everywhere.

"Jaxton," she muttered.

"Mine." And then I pressed deeper, biting down on her clit, and she came. Her pussy and her ass clamped down on me as I lapped at her, wanting that orgasm.

When she came again, the second orgasm following the first so quickly it rolled into one large one that made her back arch and a fiery flush erupt all over her body, I leaned up, hovered over her, and speared her with one thrust. Her mouth parted, a soundless shout echoing through my brain. I lowered my mouth to hers, needing her kiss, needing her.

She met me thrust for thrust as the two of us moved, arching into one another. And then I rolled onto my back, loving how she rode me like the goddess of fire she was. She put her hands on her breasts. Her hair flung back as she closed her eyes and clamped around my dick. I had one hand on her hip, the other reaching around her to press against her ass again. She cracked open one eye and gave me a smirk, but didn't tell me to stop. So, I probed her entrance, letting her lean down for a better angle, and then I was fucking her ass with my finger, my cock deep in her pussy.

When she came again, I kissed her, rolled us over so she was on her back again, and slid out of her. She let out a moan, and I flipped her onto her stomach and fucked her hard from behind with my hands gripping her hips and her meeting me thrust for thrust. I spread her cheeks, played with her ass some more, and continued pounding into her. And then something happened, something changed.

I leaned down and nibbled on her neck, and something snapped between us. It was a cord of red and blue flame that latched onto our hearts, connecting our chests.

The mating bond twisted around my soul and wrapped around hers, and I felt...everything. Her pain, her future, her need, her past. Her pleasure, her heat, her everything.

She was mine until the end of existence, and yet I knew that end could come far too soon.

She was my mate, the one who fate had chosen for me.

I hovered over her as my orgasm ended, her back still pressed to my chest, her hands clinging to the sheets.

"Jaxton," she whispered.

"I love you," I whispered, kissing her neck and then her cheek.

I kissed away her tears, the temperature of them far too hot for a normal human. She was my fire witch, and we had just mated.

I slid out of her, kissed her softly, and without words, we both cleaned each other up and showered. She piled her curly hair on top of her head as we swallowed hard to get ready for our afternoon. We had plans, and yet we needed to talk about what had just happened.

"Laurel, I didn't force you, did I?" I asked, the worry of what had just taken place taking precedence over everything. I couldn't even feel joy over the fact that I was now mated to this woman. Not yet.

Because fate had decided for us, yet I could still feel her curse tearing at the mating bond.

It wasn't complete, something was missing, and I was afraid it was because fate had decided and we hadn't.

She shook her head, tears filling her eyes again as she rose on tiptoe. She cupped my face and kissed me softly.

"Fate chose. But I killed you, Jaxton. Don't you understand that? I just killed you. I've killed you. I killed you." She kept muttering it.

I shook my head and kissed her softly. "No, you didn't. This is us. We can do this."

Sweet, blissful agony tore at my soul. I wanted this to

be better. I wanted things to change, but I wasn't sure how I was supposed to do that.

This was my mate, my everything, and yet fate had decided who we would be together.

"I killed you," she whispered.

"Damn it. Maybe this is the thing that can change it all. Maybe this is why my cousin and the necromancer came after me. Because I'm the thing that can change you. Maybe I can help us."

She looked at me then, a sad kind of hope in her gaze. "Don't hate me because I killed you."

"I love you. I fucking love you, Laurel Christopher. Don't do this. Don't hate me because you're my mate. You will not die. Neither will I. Fate cannot be that cruel to us over and over again. I have to believe that."

She rose on tiptoe again and kissed me once more. "I hope you're right. I really hope you're right." And then she held me close. I hated myself because this was the moment that I had hoped for. Had prayed for.

And the choice had been taken from us, it had been forced upon us. I didn't want her to hate me for what little time she thought we had left.

FIFTEEN

Jaxton

In the moment of peace we had while pretending we were okay, we planned a picnic lunch with my sister and Aspen. I still wasn't sure what the fae king had on his mind when it came to my sister, and I did my best not to think about that too hard.

If things were to reach the next step between them, I thought my sister would tell me. The fact that she hadn't said anything yet, however, surprised me. The relationship seemed to be far more serious than her previous boyfriend from the mer realm. She hadn't dated a hawk, and I had a feeling it wasn't because she was afraid to but because she hadn't found anyone. But she *had* found Aspen.

Nelle grinned as she laid out the blankets and sat next to Laurel on the ground. It felt surreal that we were here, Laurel and me not speaking of the mating bond or telling anyone about what had happened since we weren't sure what to say and the fact that a war was on the horizon.

In the end, however, it was all we could do to find moments of peace before another battle broke out.

"I can see in your eyes that you're thinking about what's going on outside the wards, so I should let you know that my trackers are on the northern side of the town as planned. They'll let me know if they sense anything."

I turned to Aspen and nodded, understanding that worry about what was to come was on his mind, as well. "Thank you. And, yes, that's all I can think about right now. With the additional patrols I've been taking with my team, we're doing all we can. My second and third in command are on the west side, and I know Rome is on the east."

"We have a mixture of the shifters on the south side," Aspen added.

"I know that Ash is along the edge, as well."

Laurel leaned forward. "Ash is patrolling?" she asked.

I nodded, brushing her hair from her face. "Your brother said that he wanted to try another spell. So, he's out there with a few of Rome's bears."

"Does Rowen know?"

I nodded as Nelle's gaze went between us. "Yes, she knows. I know your brother can be an asshole, but he doesn't do major spells without telling your coven sister."

Aspen frowned. "You call him an asshole to his sister's face?" he asked, confusion in his expression.

Ash's affliction, for lack of a better word, wasn't known to most people outside of our circle. And it wasn't our secret to tell.

"Ash knows it. And it's a running theme in our conversations," Laurel replied with a shrug, even though I saw the pain in her eyes. After all, I felt it along the bond, as well—one we weren't discussing.

"Enough talk of sadness. Let's talk about happy things," Nelle announced and sat close to Aspen.

"I picked up lunch. Lots of bread from Sage's bakery, and now we're going to have a picnic and pretend that the world isn't catching on fire," Laurel added quickly, and all of us laughed softly, even though there was tension to it.

"We still don't know who this Oriel is, do we?" Nelle asked.

Aspen gave her a look. "I thought you didn't want to talk about sad things?"

She huffed out a breath and shrugged. "I don't. Dad's worried too because you can connect the mer realm with this one."

"I need to talk to your dad," I said, frowning. "Maybe he knows something we don't."

"He doesn't know much, but he does want to give me the title of Emissary," she said as she rolled her eyes.

I flinched. "Because if you're the Emissary to the merpeople, then you're not part of the wing at all," I said softly.

"Pretty much. But then I would be in the know for things that you don't want me to know because you're afraid of what might hurt me."

"You're my baby sister. I'll always be afraid of what could hurt you."

"But if I have the knowledge, I can be stronger. And Aspen is teaching me how to fight."

I gave the fae a look. "I knew we discussed it somewhat, but how much are you teaching her?"

Aspen shrugged as he plucked a grape off the vine. "Your sister needs to be able to protect herself if we're not around. Of course, I taught her how to fight."

"Hey, don't get all angry with my brother. He taught me in the beginning, and Laurel taught me how to use a sword and those daggers. I'm doing better. I'm going to protect this town and our people and our families."

She gave me a pointed look, and I sighed. "I guess we're not good at talking about happy things."

"I know what would make me happy," Laurel put in.

"Oh?" I smiled at her, though weary. We were all waiting for the next shoe to drop.

"I haven't seen you in your bird form without it being in a battle in ages. Come on, fly a bit. I know you want to feel the wind beneath your wings." She teased at the joke of the song, and I flipped her off playfully.

"I don't need to preen for you like some peacock."

"No, you're a beautiful hawk shifter," she soothed. "But it's been a few days since you've flown for yourself, hasn't it? I can feel the tension."

Even as she said the words, I knew they were a mistake. Because there would only be one reason for Laurel to feel that tension.

Nelle's eyes widened. "You can feel the tension? As in a mating bond?" she asked as she clapped her hands together.

She looked between the two of us, and I sighed.

I leaned down and pressed a kiss to Laurel's cheek. "Yes, but we're keeping it between us for now. The town has other things to worry about."

My sister looked ready to celebrate or throw her hands up in the air, but one look from Aspen, who seemed to know her as a soulmate would, and she calmed down. "I'll keep the celebrations to a minimum, but as soon as you tell everybody, I'm planning the mating ceremony."

"You are, are you?" I teased.

"What? If you go with the wing, everything's going to be airy, flowy, and white. And the coven is busy with other things, so let me do it."

Laurel grinned. "You know, a goth mating ceremony might be fun. I look amazing in black."

"See? I may be the goth mermaid, but I will totally

make sure that your mating ceremony is classy, a little goth, a little sparkle, and a little flame."

I couldn't say no to the looks on Laurel's and Nelle's faces, and they knew it. "Okay, dear sister. You can help."

"I'll take it. Now, go fly. I know you need to."

I looked between my sister, my mate, and the fae king and sighed.

"Okay, but then I'm going to be hungry. Make sure you save me some food."

"Of course. I'll take care of you."

Laurel's words soothed my soul, and I stood and stripped off my shirt.

Nelle made a gagging sound before she leaped into Aspen's arms, and I shook my head before going into the copse of trees to strip down. While nudity wasn't a big deal with shifters, my sister didn't need to see. Mermaids could use their natural magic to shift their clothes into their tails. However, as a hawk, I didn't have that option.

I pulled on the anchor that was my hawk, and it called with joy as my bones broke and shifted. The agony of peace, pure joy, and ecstasy filled me. I didn't even need to touch the ground before I was soaring into the air, my wings outstretched as I found a current. I flew over my mate and family, and Laurel grinned widely as she leaned back, cradling her head with her hands as she looked up at me. Nelle leaned into Aspen as she waved, and I began to fly again. Maybe I *would* preen like a peacock, but all that mattered was that my mate and my sister were happy, and I knew I had to hope that this mating bond that fate had forced upon us would mean that there could be a future. That this wasn't the end that would change everything.

Even as I thought that, a flame licked down the mating bond. I felt the pain and sorrow in Laurel's soul. The curse was ramping up, and our frayed mating bond wasn't yet complete. It wasn't enough.

For now, we would ignore it. Just for this afternoon, at least. Just for this picnic where we could pretend.

Later, we would find a way to solve it. We would find Oriel, and our town would be safe. In this moment, I let my hawk rise to the surface, and I flew.

CHAPTER
SIXTEEN

Oriel

Oriel should have realized that this fae king would turn to the coven for help. He should have realized that the coven was far sneakier and more conniving when it came to finding their allies. But it was no matter. Though evading the fae king's trackers wouldn't be easy.

He would find a way. He hadn't been overjoyed to find that the fae king's men had nearly caught him that morning while doing his own layered spells. He'd been out in the forest, doing what he did best. He altered the secrecy and shadowed spells that would slowly deteriorate the strength and power of the so-called female witch leader. It was like acid dropping on a surface of their futures one drop at a time.

Oriel was the greatest necromancer of all time, the most powerful witch Ravenwood and the world had ever seen—would *ever* see—and he had to hide because of the fae?

Never again.

He had magic to elude them. He was good at what he did. Oriel had just been cocky. Or perhaps it was because the devious so-called leader of the witches had thought to out-think him. Oriel tapped his chin, annoyance wrapping around the immense and powerful magic in his body. Rowen's cunning wouldn't be a problem in the future. He wouldn't allow it to be a problem.

With a held-back sigh of impatience, he looked over as the hawk shifter landed in front of him and watched as William shifted back into his human form. Oriel detested shifters of any kind. They were so much harder to work with because they needed to deal with their animal forms. It never failed to annoy him that he needed to deal with their inbreeding and animalistic natures. However, William did come with an insider's knowledge to the powerful hawk wing and their determined leader, Jaxton.

When Oriel's lieutenant Renee had shown up with a mate, he'd nearly killed her right then. How dare she show up with a bond to someone else that was not him?

Not that he wanted to bed her or mate with her. He wasn't that obscene. However, he had needed her unending loyalty, and he needed to control her actions. Since her loyalties would now be divided between her mate and him, he ensured that every moment of her time was devoted to him.

If she went outside of the box in any way with that flame of hers, Oriel would strip the wings off the bastard in front of her.

He had done it once, just the feathers to see what would happen, and William had screamed in his hawk form and then again in his human form during the weeks it took him to heal. He only lived to serve Oriel, and that was something that Renee and William would know until the end of time.

Now, William was whole and healed, and Oriel's spy. He could evade the other hawks because he had history with them. William was his spy to get through the wards of the dying Ravenwood town. Once Renee and William took the next step with the revenants, he would be that much closer to taking the town.

Oriel wanted control, wanted Ravenwood's essence, because then he would be at his final stasis. The immortal he truly needed to be, to be the greatest necromancer of all time.

There was only one standing in his way. One that would have to be taken out. But he'd save her for last. He would enjoy stripping her magic from her, one morsel at a time. But first, he needed to take down those who would come against him.

First, it would have to be the dying witch and her precious hawk.

They had nearly gotten him before, but it seemed they had tricks up their sleeves. That was no bother. They would do it again and again and again. They would be no match for them.

And if that didn't work right away, they would take those who were closest to them. They would soon learn what happened when you went against Oriel and the plans in front of them.

The battle would continue, and he would be the man he needed to be. He leaned against his chair, the dead witch in front of him beginning to smell. He hated the stench of death, even though he raised the dead and controlled death itself.

"Renee," Oriel barked with a snap of his fingers. "Dispose of this one."

It was a young witch, one who had wanted to find power. They may not have wanted his type of powers, but they needed something. They had been on their way to Ravenwood, the legacy of the powerful air witch and coven too much to resist.

Oriel sneered at that. It would soon be his town they would be coming to, and they would cower before him.

Rowen didn't deserve the power she held within her veins. He would be the one in control. That, he promised himself.

"Would you like her with the other bodies? So she's ready to be a revenant?"

He nodded, shooing her away. "Yes, yes. You know what to do. Bring your mate over here. I have questions."

Renee nodded, flames dancing in her eyes. She loved to torture, enjoyed pain as much as he did, though she did nothing for him like Faith did. He missed Faith, missed how she was close to him. The way she understood him, even if she hadn't been powerful enough.

It was a pity that she was dead, but it had to happen. The prophecy said so.

At least what he knew of it. The town would fall, and he would rule. That was what the prophecy stated. The words recorded long ago at the founding of the town.

Renee dragged the girl out of the room, and Oriel looked at William.

"Tell me more about your cousin."

"What do you need to know?" William asked readily.

"I want to know how to get into the wing and how to take out Jaxton. Because once he's out, I can get the fire witch, and that's one step closer to Rowen."

William nodded, not even a moment's hesitation in giving Oriel all the details of the territory and what he thought Jaxton would do to fight.

Oriel grinned as Renee walked back in, and the battle plans commenced. The town would burn, and then the power would be his. The world would soon know what happened when they ignored Oriel for too long.

It would all burn.

And then it would bow.

CHAPTER
SEVENTEEN

Laurel

I had known the peace wouldn't last, but some part of me had wanted the time to extend. In the past two weeks, four more graveyards near the town had been ransacked. It had taken all of Jaxton's knowledge of the trade and a good deal of Rowen's magic to keep the news of the graverobbing away from the humans and media.

Oriel, William, and Renee didn't seem to care that they were endangering the secrets and lives of an entire magical civilization to get to the power and magic woven beneath the wards of Ravenwood. I wasn't sure how we would be able to keep our people safe for much longer with the constant revenant attacks.

Not only were the graves dug up, but their former occupants—at least those not cleansed by magic in the first place—were finding their way into town and terrorizing all in their path.

Renee's magic was far stronger than Faith's, and we were on the losing side of an already uphill battle.

And through it all, I could only use my sword.

The mating bond between Jaxton and I wasn't complete, and I wasn't sure it would ever be. I *knew* I couldn't let it, however. Not when I knew that I'd take Jaxton down this fiery path with me.

"You're in your head again."

I looked over at Nelle as she sat on the yoga mat next to mine and let out a small sigh. "When am I not in my head these days?" I rolled my eyes. "I'm sorry. We're supposed to be here, in the practice, focusing on our strengths and what we can do for the future."

"We are also supposed to be meditating so we can breathe through whatever might be on our minds. Do you want to talk about it?"

I shook my head at Jaxton's sister. Since the attack on Jaxton and subsequently our partial mating, Nelle and I had gotten closer. It wasn't that Nelle and I had been adversaries before this. It was more that I had done my best not to focus on what I couldn't have, so the two of us hadn't truly been friends before this, other than liking one another. Now, it seemed as if we were both running out of time, though I didn't know what was on Nelle's mind, nor what was troubling her. I worried that it was something she was keeping from Jaxton. Jaxton knew his little sister was worried about something, and not just the constant battles or what might be coming next for the town. But Jaxton was unlike any other big brother that I knew. He purposely stayed out of Nelle's way until she needed him. I had watched just the night before when Nelle came up to him without any words, and he had held her close. Words weren't needed. His little sister had wanted a hug but didn't want to talk about what was on her mind. And yet, I knew the moment Nelle looked as if she were ready to open up, he would pry out any needs she had.

Because that was the kind of man he was. The type who wouldn't push or take but would always be there.

At least until my mating bond with him killed him.

Fire slid up my arm, and I let out a cooling breath, telling myself I needed to be stronger than this.

"Your fire is acting up again. Do you need me to get Rowen?"

Resentment bubbled up, and I told myself I needed to stop those feelings. I didn't hate Rowen. I never had. And I couldn't be jealous of her power or her control because my lack of both was what was slowly killing my oldest friend.

I shook my head, ignoring the pain in my heart that had nothing to do with the flames. "No, I'm controlling it for now. But this is probably why I need to meditate."

Nelle searched my face for answers, though I didn't have any. That was the whole reason we were in this mess, wasn't it?

"Okay, then. We're going to close our eyes, focus on the practice. Deep breath in through your nose and out through your mouth."

I did as Nelle instructed, the two of us focusing on what we could.

The fact that we were doing this on the wing grounds rather than closer to her pond or even my home worried me. It wasn't that I was afraid, not when Jaxton was near and nobody in the wing would harm either of us. It was more that things felt *off* now. Ever since the attack on Jaxton by his own cousin and the fire witch necromancer, the wing had been treating me as if I were a leper.

Perhaps I was. After all, I was dying, and they all knew it. They were just afraid that I would take their beloved wing leader with me.

Too bad for them I was far more afraid of doing that than they could ever be.

I had to hope that I would be stronger than they believed so I could protect Jaxton.

Flames licked at my fingertips, and I let out another cooling breath, telling myself I needed to focus. Not on the wing, or the resentment, and not on the ending.

I tugged on my power, wrapping it like a tight coil around my soul as it slowly eased in and out. I sensed a wild energy there, not of flame and fire, but of earth and air.

It was Jaxton, and he was mine.

My lips quirked into a smile as I felt his hot anchor glide up the bond, just a tease at the flames. My power didn't hurt him but rather tangled with his hawk without touching, and then the two separated.

Tears pricked the backs of my eyes, and I told myself that this was fine. This could be all I needed.

It wasn't that I wanted anything more. I couldn't have anything more.

But this was my future. Or it could have been.

Now, I didn't know what it was or who I would be.

In through the nose and out through the mouth with the pain and the breath.

I focused on what I could and could not hold and what I could and could not be. Nelle lay beside me as we moved into our next pose, and she talked me through the motions.

Nelle had her own steadiness, her own focus, but she didn't belong on these grounds as much as I didn't.

She was the daughter of a hawk, and those that were not. That meant she would never belong. And here I was, a witch of uncontrolled flame. One who was supposed to somehow belong to a wing who didn't allow outsiders. I knew it wasn't *all* hawks, and Jaxton did his best to keep the elders at bay, but the resentment of the others ached.

Something needed to change and soon, but I was afraid it would all happen at once. I worried the change would overcome us, and it would be Jaxton lying in agony as the revenants came and Oriel finally showed his face.

"Let out one last breath, and then you can open your eyes and tell me exactly why you kept growling through our meditation."

I heard the smile in Nelle's voice, even through the grumble, and I let out one more breath as she instructed and slowly lifted my lids to see the woman with kohl-ringed eyes and a wicked smile on her face. "You are so pretty."

Nelle rolled her eyes. "Stop hitting on me. You're taken."

I raised a brow. "Oh? You're taken as well, aren't you?" I hadn't broached the subject before, and I didn't know if now was the correct time, but I would try. I wanted to know what was happening between Nelle and Aspen. Not that I thought she would actually tell me.

I rolled my shoulders back and then got to my feet, rolling up my yoga mat before opening my arms. Nelle grinned and held me close. I kissed her cheek. "Thank you for that."

"Thank you. But I'm still not going to tell you about Aspen."

I rolled my eyes. "I didn't think you would. But thank you for pretending to indulge me for a moment." I paused. "If you need anything, I'm here for you."

"I know you are. I do like how you make Jaxton smile, though."

My heart twisted, and then *I* smiled. "I'm doing my best. I'm not always great at it, but I'm trying."

"Well, we can be misfits within this wing together if you'd like. I'm learning the best ways to thrive in a wing that doesn't understand me."

I winced. "We are still on their grounds. And those hawks have very keen ears."

"What do we have?" Jaxton asked as he came through the trees towards us. We were on the ground floor below the canopy of trees where the wing buildings were.

I hadn't expected to see Jaxton today since he had a meeting with the elders, as well as training for the older hatchlings' flight. Then he was on patrol and on cleanup duty thanks to a revenant attack the day before. I had opened the shop, worked the desk, did inventory, and then let my staff take care of closing. I had needed a moment to breathe and hadn't wanted to deal with coven issues or magic. I'd just needed to focus. So, when Nelle offered to do some meditation with me, I jumped at the chance, needing some time for myself. Something I used to do often, yet it felt like I hadn't been doing much at all for too long now.

I looked over at Jaxton and rolled my eyes. "I was just saying you have keen ears. Don't sneak up on us."

Jaxton leaned forward, cupped my face, and pressed his lips to mine. It was a gentle hello, a sweet nothing that meant everything. This was the moment I had wanted for ages, the moment that would break me. Yet I just had to live for it. I had to stop dwelling on what would happen, what could happen, and just be.

I knew the more I meditated, the more it might help. I held back a sneer at the thought. "You're beneath my aerie. What do you expect? I wanted to see you before I needed to head out and meet with Rome."

My senses went on alert. "What's wrong?"

He shook his head. "There doesn't have to be an issue every time I meet with my best friend."

"I don't know, lately, it feels like every time we take a step toward our future, something attacks us."

Nelle came up on my side and hugged Jaxton's other side. The three of us stood there in a little circle, and it felt like this could *be* something. I only wished it didn't have to end.

"I'm meeting with Rome to discuss some border issues, yes. Plus, my best friend wanted a beer. He's a bear. They like a good honey beer."

"And what do birds like? A fishy beer?" Nelle asked, her eyes wide. "Or maybe something with worms?"

"The mermaid is asking me if I like fish beer? What do you eat, then, sweet sister of mine?" Jaxton teased.

I grinned. "Well, whatever you like, if you want it charbroiled, I'm your girl." I snapped my fingers as flames danced between the two, just for an instant. Jaxton's eyes widened even as Nelle clapped.

"That's some decent control, mate of mine."

I ignored part of that as I wasn't ready and focused. For a moment, I breathed in and smiled. "I've had more control than usual, but it comes and goes. I don't know if it's the mating bond or the meditation, but while things still hurt, and I can feel it getting progressively worse, there are moments of clarity."

The look Jaxton gave me was so intense, I felt Nelle pulling away ever so slightly to go finish packing up our things to give us some semblance of privacy. "Then our mating is helping?"

I reached up and danced my fingers along his cheek. "I don't know, Jaxton. I do know that the attacks when they come still hurt. And that when I try to use my magic for more than just a burst like I just did, I can't control what pours out of me. I'm afraid that I will hurt someone other than myself someday. Someone other than you. I will never forgive myself if that happens."

"Maybe it just takes time. The full mating bond."

"We don't know how our partial one even snapped into place as it is. How are we supposed to know what to do to create the full one? I'm honestly not sure I want to mate with you." The hurt that crossed his features was gone in an instant, but I still felt it etched across my soul. "I only meant because I don't want to hurt you."

"I know, but sometimes the words hurt."

I closed my eyes and let out a breath. But before I could say anything, Jaxton's second came forward, Aiden growling a bit.

"What's wrong?"

"Something just feels…off, and I don't know what it is."

Jaxton stood taller, looking around the wing. "You're right. It's in the air. Get the sentries on alert. Nelle, call Rowen. Have her gather the troops."

I blinked and then closed my eyes, letting my connection to the earth and the fire within me settle upon my body. I couldn't do this often, but perhaps this close to Jaxton, this close to his source of power, I would be able to.

"You're right. Something's wrong."

"No need to call me. I'm here." We looked over at Rowen, her eyes fierce. "Something flew through the wards. I can't figure out where it came from, only that it felt as if it was coming here."

"Prepare—!" Jaxton began, and then there was a scream.

I dove for my sword as Nelle let her blades slip into her hands, her kohl-rimmed eyes narrowed. "Who was that?" she asked as Jaxton cursed under his breath.

"That was a sentry, and they only scream to alert

when someone is coming. Damn it. Nelle, get back to the aerie.”

“I can fight.”

“I can’t focus on saving you if I’m doing this.”

“Jaxton, protect your people. I’ve got Nelle.” I looked over at the other woman, who gave me a tight nod. Nelle could fight, not as well as the others, and her magic worked better underwater than it ever would on land, but she was trying.

I wouldn’t clip her wings. Just like I tried not to clip mine.

Jaxton growled under his breath, cupped my face in a hard grip, and crushed his lips to mine. “Be safe.”

“You, too.”

And then the first revenant slid through the trees.

It was grotesque, one eye falling out of its socket, the other one bulging. Its mouth was open, jagged teeth bared with tiny bits of flesh in between. It lumbered towards us, and I frowned. Not all revenants looked like this. Some looked perfectly embalmed. Infused with magic as if they had been nearly healed to look almost human and not merely former casings of themselves.

This one, though, it held a different magic. As if it were just a warning shot, and Renee or Oriel hadn’t even bothered to put their full magic in it.

“It’s a trap!” I called out, realizing what this was.

This was a revenant without full magic, and that meant others were coming.

The other witches, the bears that had shown, and Frank the jaguar in cat form were there, ready to fight.

Flames danced down my sword as my body radiated energy. So much energy. It felt almost like the mating bond. The battle energy intensified it, and I had to push it back. I had to focus on what I was doing.

Hawks slid out of the trees, in hawk form and human form, as revenant after revenant came.

At least three graveyards full of walking death came forward, and I shouted, my back to Nelle as we fought, taking out one after another. When Aspen ran through the trees and came to Nelle's side, I met his gaze, gave him a tight nod, and then went to my mate's side. The fae king would keep Nelle safe, and I knew that whatever power he held within his bonds, he would use it to protect her and this wing.

I had never known a battle to come out here. This was where the hawks kept their most vulnerable. Their hatchlings. Their elderly.

The fact that Oriel's minions could get this close told me that the wards were close to breaking. It didn't matter how much energy Sage infused it with given her growing power, or how much I tried with what I had left.

The town was killing Rowen, and the magic wouldn't be enough with whatever Oriel was doing to it.

We might not be enough.

I made it to Jaxton's side as he clawed a revenant. I used my sword to decapitate the thing, a sense of pity filling me for the human the person had once been, before I went to the next one.

Flames reached out, running down my arms, and I gripped the sword, doing my best to send the fire down the metal. Only some remained, the others wrapping around my arm, singeing me. Then it sputtered out, and I cursed.

The magic was coming harder and faster, and I couldn't stop it.

I wasn't going to be enough.

Another wave of revenants came, and I staggered as a hawk went down, and then a bear. Sage and Rome fought side by side, him in bear form as he roared, and Sage using her water magic to push at the long line of revenants.

Rowen met my gaze as she fought next to my brother. Ash looked fuller of emotion than he had recently.

He looked almost like his old self, fighting to protect Rowen and the town.

He might have changed when the spell and curse twisted him, but some part of him was still there. I had to hope for that.

Rowen was at my side in an instant, her black hair pulled away from her face, a bloody gash on her cheek. The fact that she hadn't used a spell to even stanch the wound told me that she was running out of magic, the town draining her.

"We need to block them. They're coming towards the hatchlings," Jaxton said from my side.

Rowen nodded. "One more spell. I'm sorry, but we need the coven." She met my eyes, the sense of *knowing* in her gaze almost overwhelming.

"I have enough for that," I said, hoping it would be enough. Whatever held me to Jaxton gave me some power. Hopefully, it would be enough to at least get through this.

Renee stepped forward, William at her side, and some of the hawks let out a shriek, a loud call that I knew was anger and shock. Maybe some of them hadn't believed that William was truly on the enemy's side, but it didn't matter.

He was here, and we had to stop him.

"Give up now," Renee said. "The sooner this happens, the fewer people will die. Oriel just needs your town. Once you concede, once the witches perish, Oriel will let the others live. He promises you that."

"Just give in," William cooed. "It'll be easier that way."

"You bastard," Jaxton snapped, angrier than I had ever seen him before. "How dare you betray us?"

"You didn't even want me to be part of the wing. I was nothing when I was with you. Now, I have a mate and more power than you could ever dream of. Give in to Oriel. Save the others. Don't be such a fucking coward with too much pride. Your indecisions are killing others."

"That's a lie," I shouted.

"And you are a waste of space," Renee said with a grin.

"You can't even control your power, and you're killing the wing to make it happen. You don't even have the strength to use one tiny little fire spell. All you do is rely on others, and you don't even know how to fight a revenant correctly. You are nothing. You always have been. Soon, my master will kill you. If I don't get to you first."

Rowen gripped my hand as Sage came to my other side, taking the sword from me and tossing it to Jaxton. She took my hand, and while I missed the sword, I knew we needed to do this.

"One more spell," Rowen growled. "One spell to banish."

"Your coven, your power of three is nothing. But you can try. It's all you do these days. You try."

I met Rowen's gaze, nodded, and spoke the spell we had practiced before.

"Earth, air, water, fire, bring us that which we desire. Stop this evil, purge this blight, banish this death to darkest night. Lord and Lady, ancestors, too, lend us your strength for what we must do. Take this darkness so we may be free. This is our will, so mote it be!"

Fire scorched my sides, licked my fingertips, and both Rowen and Sage fell to the ground. Ash and Rome were there to pick them up, Rowen pushing Ash away, Sage leaning into her mate. Had I burned them? Had I hurt them? I couldn't think. My whole body shook, and I looked up at Jaxton as he fought revenant after revenant, hawks falling, the other shifters and humans dying, anyone who was part of Ravenwood trying to protect it.

I needed to protect *them*. I needed to do something.

My hair burst into flames and covered my body, yet I couldn't feel it. I couldn't do anything.

I met Jaxton's gaze, and I screamed.

EIGHTEEN

Jaxton

I knew something was wrong as soon as I saw Laurel's face. Her eyes widened, her gaze pure fire. Blue and purple flames flickered in her irises, while orange and red highlighted the edges of her pupils. She was close to burnout, flameout. If we weren't careful, she would burst. And yet, I knew this couldn't be the end. Still, the flame was so close, dancing along the mating bond. I needed to stop this. I had to protect her. But how was I supposed to do that?

I surged forward, only to come up short as William tossed himself in front of me. "Hello, dearest wing leader."

"Why are you doing this?" I called out, my gaze searching for Laurel as the others came forward to help her. We would all be too late if we couldn't get to her. Ash and Rowen were fighting revenants, Renee coming towards them as Rome shifted back to human form and fought naked next to Sage, trying to fight off the revenants as they came in droves. The spell hadn't worked. Instead, it had imploded, splitting the revenants into two camps as flame and air and water danced in abundance between the two. Right then and there, I knew we needed earth, or perhaps even the magic of the fae and the shifters. We needed something other than the broken coven that lay before me. It wasn't enough, but I couldn't focus on that.

I needed to get through William. Needed to get through the cousin that I had once loved and thought was family so I could get to Laurel. Only she stood in a tunnel of flame, yet nothing burned her. I didn't know if she was in pain, but the soundless scream erupting from her mouth called to me. I needed to get to her. I had to protect her, but first, I needed to defend my wing. How could I choose? My mate or my wing? And yet, it felt like my cousin William wasn't going to give me a choice.

"You always thought you were better than us. You were only our wing leader because of who your father was. And he died. Died and left us. Yet everyone thought you could be strong enough to be wing leader."

"The wing leader is chosen by strength and by who

comes together. I didn't get it because of my father. You know that."

"You aren't the strongest of us all. If you were, you wouldn't spend so much of your time dealing with your witch."

I blinked at him, wondering if he was serious. "Your mate is a witch. A necromancer. She raises the dead and twists their souls to do her bidding. What do you think a necromancer is?"

"Don't you dare fucking talk about my mate."

There was something wrong with him. I didn't know what it was, but something was off. William was acting weirder than usual. Maybe much like my internal magic of being a shifter helped with the mating bond and eased some of Laurel's pain, it twisted Renee's and William's souls.

"Soon, you'll understand what Oriel wants and what you won't have. But your dumb fucking bitch of a witch mate won't even make it that far." William shifted in a blink, turning to a hawk as he tried to use his talons to claw out my eyes. I shot forward with the sword, slashing through William's chest as he let out a shriek. On the other side of the elemental wall, Renee screamed before fire rained down on us all. Ash cursed. He threw up his hands as a wall of earth came forward, and Rowen did the same, her air pushing the flames back. Sage had her hands deep in the dirt, her entire body shaking as she pulled water from the stream a hundred feet away. It slammed into the fire wall that Renee pushed.

And yet, Laurel stayed within the funnel of fire, pushing out flames in bursts towards revenants, but she seemed frozen in an ember in time.

I felt her within the mating bond and knew this was the end.

It had to be. I tossed the sword to Aspen as he fought with my sister, and I had to pray that he could help her.

I looked towards Aiden, my jaw tight. "The revenants are retreating. Get to the hatchlings."

"I understand." And Aiden did. Because my second had lost his mate, and I knew the broken shell of a man that had left behind.

He understood what I was doing.

Rowen and Sage scrambled to get to Laurel, but they couldn't penetrate the flames, even as Rome and the others continued beating down the last of the revenants. I jumped over a fallen body, an unrecognizable revenant who had once been human, and kept moving forward.

Ash pounded his hands on the flames, blood pouring down his arms. Black, charred burns appeared on his palms as he kept pushing, trying to get to his sister.

For a man who had lost everything, someone with no future and a curse that was breaking him just as much as it was breaking his sibling, I saw the boy he had once been. The one who had put everything forth to try to protect those he loved.

Ash met my gaze, and I knew he understood. So did Rowen and Rome. I didn't think Sage got it yet, but she would.

I jumped, turning into my hawk in an instant, knowing that my animal would protect my mate thanks to our bond. I couldn't say how I knew, but the bond was the only thing of truth in my head at the moment. I sliced through the flames before shifting back into human form and pulling Laurel close.

She looked at me, her body shaking, her eyes wide.

"The curse, it activated. I don't want to hurt you. I don't want to hurt anyone."

I cupped her face and wiped away her steaming tears. "It's okay. I'm here."

"But your wing. Your people."

"They'll be okay."

"No, no." She beat on my chest, even as the fire danced on our skins. It burned, though muted as if Laurel were doing everything in her power to protect me.

"It's okay, Laurel. It's okay."

It wasn't. I was going to watch the love of my life burn. Watch her fall to embers. But I couldn't let her do it alone.

"You don't get to kill yourself," she screamed.

"I'm not. If you use our mating bond, we can keep the fire and curse within the wall. We won't hurt anyone else. But you can't do it alone. Use me. We can protect the town."

It was as if I had always known this would be where it would end. And as Laurel screamed, I held her close, and the fire ignited.

Agony, sweet and blissful, rode our skin as the flames came closer and closer before engulfing us both. I looked down at the love of my life, the woman who would forever be mine, and smiled.

Because her power was a thing of beauty. It was a sweet ecstasy and strength that would bring a future. Though this could have been the ending, I knew it wasn't. This was only Laurel's beginning. I felt it through the mating bond; in the magic that pulsed around us.

And then there was only darkness. Only peace.

As I lay beneath the ashes, as others still screamed and shouted, sounding a world away as the curse unfolded, I looked up at the woman in front of me. The one who rose into the air, her wings aflame and burning brightly.

She was a phoenix.

A Christopher.

She *was* power.

For me, was this a beginning? Or an ending?

All I knew was darkness. Only peace.

Laurel

The air blew through my hair, and flames cascaded down my arms. I tilted my head to the sky and tried to see the person who would not be there.

I saw no hawk. I would see no shifter coming toward me, holding me in his arms as he relished the fact that the curse was breaking, day by day, ash by ash.

Jaxton was gone.

I had killed him.

"Laurel, come inside."

I shook my head at Sage's demand, trying to formulate thoughts and words other than a deep sigh.

"I should stay out here. Just in case."

Just in case.

As if Jaxton could actually come back.

He wouldn't be able to. We all knew it. Nobody remained in the ring of burnt ember and ash. He wasn't there. He had been taken, either by the magic or maybe by me, I didn't know.

But in the aftermath of the revenant attack and my ascension for lack of a better word, he was gone.

And I wasn't sure how I was supposed to move on.

"Laurel. Come inside. We're not done looking for him. He's not gone."

I looked over my shoulder at Rowen and raised a brow. "Are you sure about that? It feels like he's gone. We can't see him. Once the flames died down and I stood there in all my newfound phoenix power, he was gone."

"But it's magic. Magic so old that most of us had forgotten it even existed." Rowen raised her chin in defiance. "There's still a chance."

"Not if you look at the hawks. They kicked us off their land. They banished all of us, not just me. The wing blames me for killing their wing leader."

"They're hurting, but they don't know what happened. Nobody does. We have to hope."

I looked at Rowen closer then and wondered just how much hope she could have left. She had lost her connection to the love of her life. She'd lost her family one at a time until she was the only one left standing, the last of her line. She was the final Ravenwood, the one forced to put more of herself into keeping the town safe. The one who seemed to be in a losing battle to do so.

I was afraid to wonder how much of herself she had left for whatever came at us next.

"I don't know if I have any hope left to give. He wasn't supposed to die. He was supposed to let me save him. But that was Jaxton. He always had to be the one to save everyone else and never think of himself. The one time others thought he might be thinking of himself, they shunned him and tried to keep him away from me because they didn't think I was good enough for him."

"The hawks don't understand what's going on." Sage sighed. "Not that we know much more than they do. But we're going to try. We're not giving up. We all knew going in that something could happen to us. Jaxton knew what he was doing."

"Did he? He said that the bond we were slowly creating would save the town from my implosion, yet I couldn't do it myself. He's gone. And I'm somehow supposed to be okay with that? Somehow supposed to move on and fight to protect the town when no one wants me here?"

"Stop saying that," Rowen snapped. "You think you're the only one in pain? Do you think you're the only one who lost someone? Look at us. Nobody is left unscarred or unmarred. But you are still standing. You're a phoenix. You are a mythical being now. One with so much power running through you. I can feel you through the coven's bond. I can feel that, Laurel. Use it. Protect this town. Avenge Jaxton, if that's what it comes to. But we don't know that he's dead. We don't." Rowen's eyes narrowed, magic swirling around her, and I knew she was grieving just as I was, though neither of us could say it.

"I don't know where we go from here." Sage looked between Rowen and me. "I only know that we need to go somewhere. We can't stand here and wish. We can't find Oriel or even uncover a trace of who he is or what he wants beyond the town's power."

"And why? Why does he want this? *Why* is he using so much of his magic against us and yet not actually being a part of it? We don't even know if this guy exists." Rowen shook her head, then pulled her hair back from her face into a messy bun on her crown. "All we know is people keep telling us that he's the bad guy. That he's the one who keeps sending his minions to us. But we really know nothing. And that's killing me. I want to know who he is, what he wants, and whether he exists or not."

I bit my lip. "I need to do that, too. I need to get over my pity party and help." I slid my hands over my face and let out a scream. "I've been so lost in what could happen for so long. I don't even know who I am anymore. I was a warrior. The one who could use flame and my sword to fight for those who needed me. Yet all I've been doing is wallowing. I'm sorry." Hot tears burned my cheeks as I moved forward and took Rowen's hand, then Sage's. "I'm sorry. I don't know what I'm supposed to do. Things hurt, and I don't know who I am. I don't know what it means that I'm a phoenix now."

"Aren't phoenixes supposed to fly?" Sage asked softly, and my heart broke. I swallowed hard. "Maybe. But flying was for *him*." My voice broke. "Flying was for Jaxton. Why isn't he here? Why did he sacrifice himself for this town? It should have been me. It always should have been me."

"Well, with the way we keep getting attacked in our small town, it just might be the case soon."

I winced. "I need time to think. To breathe. I'll be back, I promise. To practice with the coven now that I have this new power. Now that I know I won't kill myself and burn every time I need to use it. But it's hard to think that every time I need to pull on the flame, I know it's because of Jaxton. And he's not here. I just need a moment." My hands shook, but I could see that Rowen got it.

I wasn't weeping. I wasn't flailing on the ground, wishing for what I couldn't have.

I might be broken, but it was anger that coursed through my veins. And if I weren't careful, if I didn't rein it in, along with the new power pulsating through my soul, I would hurt. Not myself but others.

And I had already taken Jaxton with me, even if he had done what he had always said he would do: protect the town with everything he could. I couldn't do more than I already had.

"Go. Breathe. Then come back to your sisters. The

town needs you. We need you. And we don't know that he's gone, Laurel. Not forever. Just remember who you are and who needs you."

I swallowed hard and then pulled away from the girls, my entire body ready to break. I passed the alley behind our buildings, moved through the trees, got as close as I could to a sense of peace and normalcy. That didn't exist, did it? It never would again.

Once the battle had died down, and the others had taken care of any revenants that got through, and William and Renee had slithered away like the demons and cowards they were, the wing had taken one look at me and turned their backs. It was as if they knew this would happen. And maybe they had. Maybe we all had. Maybe we understood that I would be the death of their wing leader, the end of the man I loved.

They wouldn't talk to me now, and I knew there would need to be serious contemplation of who would be the next wing leader once they finally allowed themselves to grieve Jaxton's death. I wanted to know exactly how they would fight within the aerie.

Would they run away? Would they save themselves and leave Ravenwood? It wasn't as if the elders hadn't wanted to do that already, for longer than I cared to admit.

If the wing left Ravenwood, that would lower our defenses. But maybe that was for the best. If Oriel came for the town's magic, maybe keeping the hawks indeed safe and away from the town itself was the only way.

I couldn't focus, couldn't think.

All I could do was see Jaxton's face as he looked at me with peace and hope as if he were going to wait for me on the other side. Only I hadn't followed him.

And then his face melded to Nelle's, and I saw the anger etched on her features.

Aspen had taken her away, though not to the wing. I wasn't sure if she would ever be welcome there again, not without Jaxton's presence. Another nail in my coffin.

I didn't know if Nelle had gone back to her people in the water or to the faes' compound on the other side of town. I had never stepped foot on that land, as it hadn't been my place. Though Rowen had, and now Ash as well.

I had seen the accusation on Nelle's face. I knew she blamed me. She couldn't blame fate. Why not the person who had actually burned him?

Anger erupted from me, and my toes lifted from the ground, giant, fiery wings erupting from my back. I threw my head back and screamed, flames dancing and winding around me as if I had been born for this purpose.

I was a phoenix, and I had no idea what my powers were. I only knew it would take years for me to grow into them and learn what I could do.

The anger within me broke, and I pushed forward, my flames pouring into the tree in front of me.

If it was a decayed one, one not long for this earth,

then the disease on it had to be excised before it hurt the others around it.

Just like I was a disease to my coven.

The tree burned before falling to ash and soot.

I fell to my knees, tears sliding down my cheeks as I mourned.

No matter what Rowen said, Jaxton wasn't coming back.

I had been born again through flame, and he had been the sacrifice the fates needed for the coven to have my power.

I didn't know if I could forgive myself for that.

"Having fun burning things? Knowing that you're never going to be strong enough?"

I whirled, my hand going for my sword, only to find it wasn't there. I always had my sword on me, and yet I had left it behind.

So quick, I was relying on my powers—ones I didn't know if I would ever fully control—instead of the blade that had served me well for so long.

I stood, balls of flame in my palms as Renee shook her finger at me. "I only want to talk, little phoenix. I don't want trouble."

"You constantly attack our town, and you say you don't want trouble?"

"I haven't hurt you, have I? No, the world seems safe enough. Your little town isn't on fire. And we both know I could do that. After all, aren't you the one who can burn this town to its final beams and twigs before you walk away unharmed? I can feel the power burning within you. Wouldn't it be wonderful if you could control it?"

"What do you want, Renee?"

"I want you to know that there is a way to control it. Though you're not going to like the answer."

"I'm not using dark magic and becoming a necromancer to control this," I spat. "I am a phoenix. I am a fire witch. And I am coven. I am stronger than you will ever be."

Renee threw her head back and laughed. "Oh, you're laughable. I mean, really? You've never been stronger than me."

"I don't even know you."

"Of course, you do. Don't you remember the little witch who came to town when you were a little girl? You never noticed me. No, you only wanted to play with your best friend and your brother. You trailed around after that little hawk boy and the little bear that I don't see around town. Didn't you wonder if it hurt when he died? I hear Faith rose him from the dead again, another revenant to play with. I'm only sad that I wasn't there to see it and be a part of it."

My hand shot out, flames speeding towards her. Renee flicked it off as if she weren't even trying hard.

"I'm not done talking. We can play later."

"All of this because I didn't play with you when you were a little kid? I don't even remember you."

"Of course, you don't. Because your precious coven already had a fire witch. They didn't need two."

"We weren't even a coven back then." I didn't even remember this woman. But, apparently, I had hurt her in some way. "I'm sorry if I hurt you. Truly. But we were children, if what you're saying is true. We weren't a coven. We hadn't come into our magic. When did we meet?"

"Outside the café that's no longer there. Apparently, it burned down in a fire when we were five or so."

She winked as she said it and my stomach rolled. "You were five when you burned that down?" I remembered the little café with its dark, iron tables and happy pink colors. They'd had cupcakes and sandwiches and after-noon tea for those who wanted it.

And it had burned to the ground. The owners, an older pair of witches who had just wanted to be part of a magical place, had decided not to rebuild.

They had moved away a few years after, wanting to be closer to their children, who hadn't been born with magic and hadn't wanted to live surrounded by it.

Ravenwood was dying, taking its magic with it, and I knew it was because of the curse of the town and the curse of the Christophers.

One that had pushed Sage away.

Something that had tried to kill me and had broken Ash.

Now, the curse that spoke of darkness, that warned it

would come for us and break Ravenwood open, exposing it to the darkness itself, was attached to Rowen.

And her soul was attached to the town. So when the Ravenwood broke, so would she.

We were thrice cursed, thrice broken, and I had to hope there was a way out of it. A way to breathe.

But I couldn't think about any of that right now. I had to focus on the witch in front of me.

"Fire to fire, little witch? I'd love to see you burn baby burn. You rose as a phoenix from the ashes, even though you should have died long ago from the Christopher curse. It seems that fate likes to throw us curveballs, but that is fine. You don't know your magic. And remember, I'm a necromancer. A higher one. That means I can pull revenants from spirits and bodies. I can control them all, as well as the darkness. You don't give in to that, even though you should if you want to be a true phoenix. That means I will always beat you. I am the more powerful one. You just have to remember that."

And then Renee lifted her hands, palms up, and deep shadows and fog crept over the land.

This was the fog of a necromancer. It didn't matter what element they held. It was what pushed it forward.

While Faith had been a water witch, she could also use the necromancer fog because she had tainted her soul with that darkness.

It seemed that Renee was no different.

Revenants began pouring through the fog, the shuffling echoing in my ears. I was alone out here, a situation of my own making, but I would not let these revenants or this fire bitch hurt my town. My family.

They had already taken Jaxton from me. I had already taken Jaxton. I wouldn't let them take anything else.

I shot my first fire dagger at them, slicing through one revenant. Renee clapped, dancing in place as she did a cartwheel and shot out more flame from the balls of her feet. Renee was powerful, but I would be a power.

I would avenge Jaxton's death if it were the last thing I did. I would make sure that nobody else died by a fire witch or me again.

I moved forward through the darkness, using my flame as a beacon to take out one revenant after another. They fell, their bodies broken husks. Renee wasn't using the shades, and I had to be thankful for that. To fight the revenants and the ghosts, I would need a full coven, and I wasn't there yet.

I only had to hope that Rowen felt the disturbance within the wards and would come to help.

Or...I could do this on my own. I had access to powers I hadn't before. I could do this without hurting myself or others, unless that's what I wanted to do.

I wasn't cursed anymore. The darkness that lay behind me had taken everything from me. Now, I had to look to the future. And I had to fight.

I took out another revenant and then another. Blood splattered my clothes as I moved forward, trying to get to

Renee, but she was too fast. She was pulling on the powers of a necromancer, and I knew that she would fade shortly.

While the power of a necromancer was strong, it didn't last. It fed on the witch's soul, and there was only so much soul to use before you broke completely.

Either Renee would leave once she sputtered out, or she would die. And I didn't think she would let that happen.

Revenants surrounded me, and I cursed, only just now noticing that the fog closed us in the circle.

Somehow, Renee was keeping the others from me. I was alone.

I had to be stronger than this.

Somehow.

Fire scorched my arm, and I cursed, annoyed that I got distracted by a revenant and allowed Renee to get too close.

I couldn't focus on her and the revenants simultaneously, but I had to do this. Flames erupted from my hands, and I pushed them forward, fighting back.

Suddenly, something came out of the darkness, and I nearly tripped over my feet.

Dozens of revenants surrounded me. I pushed back, fighting, trying to make it through before looking up at...Jaxton.

He was here. Whole. He'd come through the darkness alive. He winked at me and then pulled out a sword, *my* sword. I had left it at home. Or had I? Had it burned in the fire? I didn't remember. I felt like I was dreaming.

Jaxton cut down a revenant and then another, and I moved towards him, trying to get closer, needing to see if this was a mirage or something real.

Renee looked between us, her eyes wide before she cursed, and then she ran. I moved after her, but the fog thickened, pushing me back. This was magic I wasn't strong enough to fight because I wasn't a necromancer and refused to go dark. I took down the last revenant and then hurried towards Jaxton—or at least the person I thought could be him.

He was fighting, breathing. He didn't scent of a revenant.

I couldn't focus.

"Jaxton?"

He moved forward, sword in one hand as he cupped my face with the other.

I felt warmth.

This was real.

He wasn't dead.

"How are you here? Where were you?"

Wet tears slid down my cheeks, and Jaxton lowered himself a bit, his forehead pressed to mine. "I needed to come back. I'll always come back to you."

I didn't understand. I couldn't.

But I didn't care. I threw my arms around him as

flames swirled in a vortex near us. The others came forward, the spell in the fog finally breaking, and I held my mate, hoping that I didn't wake up from this dream that couldn't be a dream, from fate that didn't feel much like fate.

CHAPTER
TWENTY

Jaxton

Coming back from death when you were a wing leader, and hawk shifter meant I didn't have paperwork, but I did have to speak to a few people.

Laurel had gone back with the coven, the three of them needing to focus on Laurel's new powers. I hadn't wanted to stay away from her, the mating urge between us so intense that it was hard for me to even breathe sometimes.

Though I knew I would see her soon. There was only so much distance we could give each other when I had come back from the darkness just for her.

Now, though, I needed to speak to my wing so they understood what had happened. Not that I knew precisely.

"You're back," Aiden said as he moved forward and bowed.

I frowned at him, wondering why he was bowing to me. We did not bow to one another.

"Stand up, Aiden. Why are you doing that?"

"You're my wing leader. I'm making sure that anyone watching knows that I'm not taking your place."

I frowned, tilting my head as I studied him.

"Everyone thought I was gone. Of course, someone would try to take my place. It wouldn't have been safe for the wing not to have a leader."

Aiden gave me a look.

"You sure do seem all-knowing for a man who just rose from the dead."

"Hopefully, not completely risen," Rome said from behind me, and I snorted as my friend came forward. I might need to meet with the hawk shifters, but my best friend would not leave me alone. My best friends for that matter, considering Ash was by Rome's side. The guys were going to ensure that I didn't disappear again.

I didn't blame them for being worried. But I knew that I would want to be alone with my mate soon.

"I'm back. I will fight to see who needs to be wing leader if I need to. But I won't hurt you. Do you understand that?"

Aiden shook his head. "I was the one the elders wanted. I am the second strongest after you. But I wasn't going to take your spot."

"Well, now that we have that settled, I guess we should go speak to your elders," Ash said dryly.

I sighed. "That's not something I'm looking forward to. But first, where's my sister?"

Aiden winced. Anger rode me, and I narrowed my eyes. "What happened when I was away?" *Away* seemed like the best thing to say just then since *on the brink of death while waiting in the In Between* didn't seem like something I should approach just yet.

"She's fine. Safe. She's with Aspen."

"I came here to talk to the wing, my sister, my family, and to explain what happened. Why wasn't my sister allowed to stay with the wing?"

Aiden let out a small growl, and Rome answered it. Birds didn't growl. It was more of a gruff rumble. Bears, on the other hand, their rumbles echoed throughout the forest. Ash just looked between them and shrugged before moving on towards the wing.

"She didn't feel she would be safe with the elders because she knew they didn't want her here." My eyes narrowed, my bird of prey moving forward, wanting to slash at anyone who came towards me. "Excuse me?

"She's safe. We made sure of that. But we couldn't do that with her on the aerie premises while we were trying to figure out where to go."

"My sister is part hawk. She may only shift to a mermaid, but she is still a part of this family. I'm done with the elders and the rest of the wing thinking they can push us around because we do not conform to their ideals."

Rome's lips quirked into a smile. "Sounds like you're having problems just like my bears were." His smile wasn't nice, yet I appreciated it. "I'll help you make sure that what happened to us doesn't happen to you."

"It already did with William." I shook my head. "Come on. We'll meet with the elders later. I can't do it right now."

"Are you sure?" Aiden asked.

"I need to find my aunt. She's broken over what William did. Then I'm going to find my sister. *Then* I'm going home to my mate. When I return, I'll still be the wing leader that you need."

Of course, it seemed I wouldn't have time for what I wanted. I waited as the elders came forward. The way they bullied those not under their purview needed to stop. Now.

"Then tell us what happened," Gerald, one of the elders, said from the aerie as he moved forward. "Why were you gone? What magic is this?"

I would have forced him to submit to me as someone far less dominant, but I saw the fear in his gaze. He wasn't afraid of me but of what had happened. Maybe he needed answers, but then again, so did I. "The curse broke. Laurel is what she was always meant to be. I went with her to ensure that the town was safe from whatever backlash could hurt us. And in so doing, I went to the In Between."

Ash cursed under his breath. "And they let you out?"

I didn't even know Ash knew of the In Between, but here he was, speaking of it as if he had been there, too. I had questions for my friend, but not here, not in front of others.

"I have let this wing do what they need to feel safe. I am not the type of wing leader to throw around my power and defeat those weaker than me. I have tried to protect everyone I can while listening to their problems. And I have let you walk all over me in the process."

"Jaxton, we didn't know. There was a reason."

I shook my head at Gerald. "Have your meeting with your elders. We'll meet soon, and you will tell me exactly why you chose to disgrace who you are within this wing and who we are as a people. We are Ravenwood. We were sent here to protect those who needed it. Ravenwood should be a safe place. And it's not the witches breaking us down. It is not the magic. The way we are in-fighting is bringing our wing down. We cannot allow this to happen again. I was in the In Between, but I was still here, watching as much as I could. You pushed my sister away. You pushed me away. You won't do that again. I'm done holding your hand and trying to get you to come to the future we are in. No more. Meet with your elders, meet with your side of whatever fight you think we are on, and then come to me. You will know exactly where we need to be. I am done pretending for you. I am not submissive. I am the fucking leader of the Ravenwood wing. And we will fight the darkness. But we will no longer have darkness within ourselves. Do you understand me, Gerald?"

Gerald lowered his head and tilted it to the side to submit. "I understand, Jaxton. We'll explain. I promise."

I wasn't sure I wanted their form of explanation, but I nodded. "Fine. I'll be back tomorrow. We'll discuss it then. I've always been all-in with this wing, Gerald. I regret that you haven't seen that but know that the wing is part of the town. The fact that you haven't seen that for so long is on your shoulders and mine. We will not have that again."

Gerald nodded again, then he walked away, Aiden following. "I'll make sure he gets home."

And that was the wing we should have been. Aiden, as a dominant, helping the more submissive Gerald find his way home to be safe.

When they disappeared, that left me with my two friends as they stood on either side of me, Rome giving me a look I had never seen before, and Ash looking far off into the distance. I had to wonder what was wrong.

"I need to find my sister. And then I need to go to my mate."

"I'll stay with your wing," Ash put in.

I blinked. "Really?

"To ensure that nobody decides to try to take out your

wing leader back from the dead and because they are hurting.”

“You can feel their hurt?” Rome asked, voicing my question.

Ash gave a small smile, but it didn’t reach his eyes. “I don’t know anymore. And that’s the problem, isn’t it?” And then he left to follow where Aiden and Gerald had gone, leaving us standing there wondering what would happen to our friend once there was nowhere left to hide and no one left to fight for.

“I’ll go watch the coven and do what I do best. You find your sister.”

“No need,” Aspen said from the trees as he came forward. Nelle was at his side, and she gave me a look as if she were studying me to make sure I was real. And then she ran. I held out my arms, and she jumped into them, before settling back, her body flashing from her fin to her legs again.

I shook my head, kissing her hard on the forehead before holding her close. “You must be freaking out if you can’t hold your shift.”

“Shut up. You died. You really died.”

“I’m back. I promise. And I wasn’t dead. I was more in stasis. Waiting.” It seemed like the only thing I could say just then since nothing made sense when it came to magic.

“I’m glad you’re back, wing leader,” Aspen said softly. “It wasn’t time for you to leave us.”

I hated when the fae king got all mystical like that, but I didn't say anything since I agreed with him.

"Never leave me again. I was so mad. So broken." Nelle closed her eyes tightly and leaned against me as I held her close. "I'm sorry. For everything. I'm going to find our aunt and hold her and tell her I'm sorry for what William did. I hate what happened. And when you find Laurel, make sure she knows that I'm sorry, too. And then I'll tell her."

I froze and moved away. "Why do you need to apologize to Laurel?"

Nelle ducked her head, her pale cheeks reddening. She didn't have her kohl eye makeup on. Instead, her hair was piled on the top of her head, and she looked far younger and more innocent than I had ever seen her. "I didn't say anything mean to her, but I *was* angry, and I took it out on her. I walked away. I didn't want to talk to her. I'm sorry."

I closed my eyes and cursed. "You'll be telling her that to her face. But Laurel will understand. She loves you."

"I love *you*, big brother. But never do that again."

She held me close, and I looked over her head at Aspen. The fae king looked at my little sister as if she were his entire world, and I raised my chin. "When it's time, you and I will have a discussion, too."

My sister punched me in the ribs, and I rolled my eyes as Aspen just smiled. The fae leader looked forward. "I figured as much. Maybe it's time that both of us stopped waiting in the wings as it were and moved forward to keep our town, our people, and our...families intact."

And with that, Aspen pulled my sister away, and they moved in the direction Ash had gone.

I shook my head and looked at Rome. "I wasn't gone for that long, was I?"

"Three days is a long time when it comes to death and losing those you love. Go to Laurel. She's waiting." Rome rubbed his chest. "I can feel Sage waiting for me."

I put my hand over my heart, the small mating bond between Laurel and me barely warming.

I was not a phoenix. I could not turn to flame like my mate could, but I *could* bolster her power like she could ramp up my strength. We were two sides of a coin and would forever be entangled. Now I knew we had a chance to fight Renee, William, and Oriel. To protect our town.

I gave Rome a nod, stripped off my shirt, and shifted. It felt so good. As if I'd been waiting for this for eons, and yet it had only been a few short moments. The wind billowed beneath my wings, and I found a stream to glide over the trees and around the forest dotted with small homes. Finally, I headed toward Laurel's place. My other home. Or perhaps it was just *she* who was my home.

I landed on the back porch and shifted to human, making my way naked to the back door. Laurel opened it quickly and threw herself at me. I held her close, letting her pepper my face with kisses as she grinned at me, her eyes bright. There were still flames within them, and the scars on her side from the curse might never fade, but it didn't matter. I kissed her hard on the mouth, holding her close.

"You're naked, and I don't care. I mean, I like that you're naked."

I smiled against her. "I've missed you."

"I know you had to go see the wing and your family, but I don't want you to ever leave my side again. How can you be here?"

I walked her inside the house and closed the door behind me as I just held her close. "I don't know how I'm here, other than the In Between didn't want me."

Her eyes widened. "You were in the In Between?"

"It was dark. As if the darkness that came from the necromancers pulled me in but didn't know I could get out. I don't know how I knew where I was, other than knowing I could leave when it was time. And seeing you fighting, seeing Renee come at you like that?" Even as I said the words, anger filled me. "I knew it was time. I didn't know how much time had passed, and I was worried it had been too long, but then I was able to come to you. Because I was there for you. As you will always be there for me. I feel like we've wasted so much time waiting to see who we could become, but I don't want to wait anymore, Laurel. I love you. You're mine, and I love you."

She lowered her feet to the floor as she cupped my face and kissed me again. "I love you, too, Jaxton. And you're mine. I was so afraid for so long. I don't want to be afraid anymore. I want to fight by your side, live by your side, and just be yours. I can feel you here." She put her hand over her chest. "In my heart. And I know that mating bond is still there, even though I couldn't feel it while you were in the In Between."

"But I'm no longer there. I'm here. And I'm stronger than I was." Not just in physical strength, but in who I could be. "We're going to fight. We're going to win. And I'm not going to lose any more of my wing or this town to this fucking necromancer who thinks they can take us."

She grinned at me. "I love when you get all dangerous and growly. Makes me hot."

"Good, because you're far too clothed."

I pulled off her shirt and tugged down her sweats, leaving her bare to me. I dropped to my knees as she widened her eyes, and I spread her. "Hold onto something, mate of mine. Things are about to get steamy." And then I latched my mouth to her pussy and sucked.

Laurel slid one leg over my shoulder as I kissed her intimately, needing her taste, just needing *her*. We were standing in her living room, and I felt as if I were living outside myself, watching me make love to the woman I loved. When she came on my face, I stood and kissed her again, needing her.

"That's a way to say hello," she muttered against my lips as I picked her up and slowly carried her to her bedroom.

"I've missed you," I murmured.

"I've missed you, too. I feel like I've been missing you all of my life, afraid to want you more than I already do." I soothed away her tears as I laid her down on the bed before gently nipping at her lip and kissing her again and again. "I don't want to live for the past or even tomorrow. I want to live for right now."

I smiled and kissed her one more time. "It's just you and me." Even as I said that, I knew it wasn't completely true. We would always miss Trace. The person who was our best friend and could have possibly been more. But fate had decided against it. However, it was the two of us now, and I wasn't letting anyone take her away from me. Not a curse, not even death itself. She was my flame, and I was her spark. And the world would have to get on board with that.

I left gentle nips between her breasts as she lay back and let me love her. And when I licked her burn scars, she smiled down at me, no fear in her eyes this time, just promises of a future that was ours. I shifted, my hand still between her legs as I gently brought her to climax again. And then I settled between her open thighs, met her gaze, and entangled my fingers with hers.

"Ready?" I whispered.

"Always. Please. Be mine." As I kissed away her tears again, I slid deep inside her, both of us groaning at the feeling.

I rolled to my back, letting her take control. I didn't

mind. Because right here, we were only Laurel and Jaxton. I might not be the growly predator shifter that people thought I needed to be, but I was still a leader, still dominant. But this woman, my mate, was my equal. My everything.

I would burn down the world for her. We had nearly done that for each other. And now as she rode me, my balls tightening and my dick hard, I knew that this was only the beginning. It had to be.

The mating bond snicked into place between us, my hawk gliding over the bond towards her flame. Her phoenix danced with my anchor, and my eyes widened as she grinned.

"Whoa," she whispered, and then she came again. I clung to her, both of us rolling to the side as we held each other.

Those attacking the town would come for us. I knew it. But for now, I would simply hold my mate and know that we had gotten our second, third, and infinite chance.

I had promised myself I would never stop trying. And I wouldn't. Yet I knew this was it. It had to be.

I had died once for Laurel, and I would do it again. But if fate shined down on us, with the curse fully gone, our mating bond would be forever. And death was only our beginning.

CHAPTER
TWENTY-ONE

Jaxton

Magic pulsated within the bookshop, and I leaned against the doorway, my gaze on my mate and my family.

Though the curse had broken for Laurel, it hadn't for the others. Darkness still surrounded the town, and Ash was still dealing with his personal scourge. For now, I knew the coven in front of me was doing their best to focus on what they could fix and what they could change.

We hadn't had a revenant attack since I came back from the In Between. I didn't know if that was Oriel and Renee regaining their composure and gathering their forces or if it was just them playing with us. Knowing how

William had been when we were kids, it felt like a cat and mouse game. That they were waiting for us to make the next move, even though we didn't have one.

Rome pulled up next to me and frowned. "Ariel and I were out on the eastern section this morning because Rowen thought she felt a disturbance in the wards, but there was nothing." Ariel was Rome's beta, having taken Trace's place when Faith killed the other bear. She was strong, smart, and knew how to fight. She was also a damn good tracker.

"If she couldn't find anything, maybe it was nothing."

"Yes, maybe it was a small bunny making that disturbance." Rome shook his head. "No, somebody wanted us out there. Maybe to test our defenses again?"

I frowned, pulling out my phone.

Me: *Aiden, any breaches?*

Aiden: *No, we're on alert. Getting ready for this evening as well. However, there have been no sightings. No ward breaks on our end. Yours?*

I had left Aiden in charge while I went to the witches today to go over spells and plans with the coven. Aiden was to track any encroachments onto our territory, just in case William had found a way in. After all, he had once known the land as well as we did. And no amount of changing access points and increasing security could change the fact that William had grown up in the aerie and knew it like the back of his hand.

Me: *Keep on the lookout. Something's happening, or at*

least it's coming, and we don't know what it is. The coven is doing a healing spell today to help strengthen the wards now that Laurel is back. Hopefully, that will help.

Aiden: *Sounds good to me. We'll take all the help we can get. The hatchlings can't wait to see you guys.*

My lips quirked into a smile.

Me: *Good. I can't wait to see them.*

I slid my phone back into my pocket and turned around. Rome did the same with his cell, and we leaned in to each other, trying not to interrupt the coven.

"Anything?" Rome asked.

"No, but Aiden's on the lookout. And they're getting ready for this afternoon."

Rome grinned. "Sounds like a plan." His anchor moved around his neck and then down his arm, as my hawk did the same on mine. His bear was so playful, even if it was a bit of an asshole sometimes. But it liked my hawk as if they—and Rome and I—had been friends and brothers since the beginning of time. And sometimes, it felt like that.

"Are you done?" Ash asked as he came over to us. He wasn't part of the spell today, and I wasn't sure if he felt put out about that or not. I didn't know if he felt anything.

"We are. They haven't started the spell yet. We aren't interrupting them," Rome grumbled, and I held back a smile.

Rowen looked over at us, her long, dark hair pulled

back from her face. "We're about to do the spell, so I'm going to need quiet. From all of you." She glared at Ash, even though he was the one who had spoken the least, but we knew why that was. We all knew, but I wasn't sure Ash knew anymore.

Now that Laurel had broken her curse, I wanted to focus on not only keeping the town safe from whatever darkness was coming, but also Ash.

William was a problem. We would deal with him. Just like we had dealt with Alden, we would deal with my cousin and his betrayal. But I also wanted to fix Ash. Not that he thought he was broken. And that was the problem. But he was. Something had irrevocably shifted within him, and we needed to fix it. That meant breaking down barriers and hurting people along the way. And I didn't know if any of us were truly ready for that.

Ash settled on Rome's other side, and we leaned against the wall, watching our three women.

They stood in a circle after Laurel let her hair down. It cascaded down her back, all long waves and blunt bangs. Laurel's reddish hair curled around her face as she hadn't straightened it that morning, and Sage's honey brown hair floated in a wind that wasn't there but perhaps was all Rowen's magic.

They were the coven, the three, the power.

We were the supports, and I knew that. Rome knew that. I didn't think Ash did. Or perhaps, as an earth witch, it was his duty to be part of the coven and they wouldn't let him. I didn't know but that was something we would likely have to focus on next.

"We will call forth the spell of healing to strengthen the wards. It'll be two-fold, and those connected to us might feel the pull against the bonds." Rowen met my gaze, the same as Laurel before Rowen and Sage looked towards Rome.

Nobody looked at Ash.

The women held hands as they spoke.

"*Magic mends while candles burn, sickness ends and health returns. Harm to none, this we decree. This is our will, so mote it be!*"

Warmth tingled inside the bond, and my hawk flew against it, dancing with Laurel's fire phoenix. I smiled, heat suffusing me as if I were the one being healed, not aiding by adding my energy and bolstering what strength she had.

Once the girls finished speaking, Laurel turned to me and grinned before they turned back to one another.

"And now, the wards."

"*Powers of the witches rise, fly unseen across the skies. Lend courage and might to those we love, with helpful strength from all above. With these words we seal this place, wards will flare with all due haste. Sealed within, we do decree, Raven-wood is safe, so mote it be!*"

The bonds that signaled me as wing leader strengthened, the energy pulsing as I stood, on alert. Rome did the same, but Ash froze, his body going pale. As soon as

Rowen stopped speaking, she closed the circle and ran towards Ash, cupping his face. I wasn't even sure she was aware she was doing it until her hands dropped suddenly, and she stood straight. "Did that hurt you?" she snapped.

Ash shook his head, even though sweat beaded on his temples. I knew it had. "I'm fine."

"That's a lie. We know that."

"Don't lie to me," Rowen whispered, the emotion in her voice pulling at my hawk. Laurel's hand slid into mine as Sage leaned against Rome, and we watched the two in a tableau, unable to do anything.

That protection spell had tried to attack Ash. And that was worrisome for more than one reason. However, we were going to do what we did best and not talk about it. Yet.

I leaned down and brushed my lips against Laurel's, then pulled out my phone. "We need to head over to the wing soon."

Laurel gave me a worried gaze then looked at her brother before sighing. "Yes, we do."

"This is our one chance for normalcy before we take the fight to them."

"I know. I just don't think the wing wants to do this."

I grumbled, knowing she might be right. "We're going to make sure they understand exactly what is going to happen in the future. And we're going to enjoy it."

She grinned. "I like when you get all growly. It's sexy."

"I told you growly is sexy," Sage singsonged.

Rome, the big alpha bear, blushed. "Stop it, woman."

I laughed, feeling almost normal, even though nothing was. Not with Renee, William, and Oriel still out there.

But we would take the fight to them. It was time.

But first, we needed to meet with the wing and celebrate the mating that had been a long time coming.

We met with the elders under the sun in the field below the wing. While the homes and the actual aerie were above in the trees, we had a welcoming spot for those who weren't of the wing and didn't want to be so high. It was easier for us to all gather and celebrate in more than just bird form.

I checked on our newest resident, the hatchling I had helped to bring into this world. The baby slept on my chest for a while, Laurel giving me an odd look. And then it hit me. I had never thought about being a father, not because I didn't want to be, but because the person I had wanted to have a future with thought she wouldn't have one.

This could be something now. Eventually. First, we needed to defeat the necromancer and save the town. But maybe a future could include a little fire hawk.

I smiled, kissed the baby on top of her soft, downy head, and handed her over to her mother. I held a few other toddlers, played around with some of the teens, and had Laurel at my side for most of it.

Introducing her as the wing leader's mate was far

different from a coven member or just a friend. People would have to get used to her at my side. And perhaps, they were.

Aspen and Nelle stood off to the side, speaking with Rowen. My sister looked animated. I smiled at the sight, knowing Nelle was in good hands with Aspen, even if I still didn't know the true nature of their relationship.

Elijah came forward, along with Gerald and Edgar, three of the elder leaders. They were their own council and didn't necessarily speak for the entire wing, but they had caused enough problems recently that I was ready to kick them out. When Laurel squeezed my hand, I let out a breath and did my best to breathe.

Looking forward, Elijah bowed his head.

"Your mating party is quite a hit," the elder spoke softly.

I tilted my head. "It's long overdue." I squeezed Laurel to my side and kissed the top of her head. I could practically feel her roll her eyes even though I couldn't see her face. "Our wing is here, as well as the pack, the coven, some fae, and many members of our town." I knew I was just stating the obvious, but I didn't give a flying fuck.

"I understand." Elijah let out a breath before Gerald spoke again. "Long ago, there was a prophecy."

I froze as the others of our small crew came forward and listened in. I wasn't sure I would like what he was about to say.

"It was said that a fire witch would remove our

strength. That they would mate into the wing and kill our members. That they would cause our wing to fall."

Laurel sputtered at my side, and I narrowed my eyes.

"Why wasn't I told any of this?"

"We couldn't say anything. The prophecy said we couldn't. That those who could take down our wing could not know."

"So you tried to what? Push away anyone who wasn't hawk in order to protect the wing? That doesn't make any sense." I growled, just like Rome. "That's why you never wanted me to be friends with Rome or Trace. That's why you don't want me helping the coven. Because you were afraid if I did, if *we* did, it'd take down the wing itself?"

Gerald had the grace to blush while Edgar ducked his head. "It seems we were wrong. That it was Renee, the fire witch, who took William and tried to take down our wing. We were wrong."

Then it hit me. Yes, a fire witch *had* taken a member of our wing as her mate. I let out a breath. "We will not let those two nor Oriel destroy us. We are stronger together."

I looked around at the rest of the party. As the music died down, everyone looked at us. Even the hatchlings looked at us. And I figured it was time for them to listen. Everyone needed to be on the same page, and I needed to stop placating the elders and their damn prophecies that had been hidden from us for so long.

"Our wing has a long way to go to get into the future we need it to be. But we are working on it. We are finding our place within this town that isn't hidden within the trees. All of us are touched by those who are not hawk, and we need to remember that." I looked at my sister as she leaned into Aspen. "My sister is mermaid and hawk, and yet we treat her as if she's an abomination. We're done with that. There are others among us who aren't full-blooded hawks. Who found mates of fate and heart outside these walls. It's time we remember that we are part of this town and part of the greater magic of Earth. Not just hidden within the feathers of what we thought we needed to be. We will be strong. We will be strong enough to take down the darkness. To take down Oriel."

I let out a breath. "We will never let what happened to William happen to anyone else." My aunt watched me, but she didn't flinch, didn't pale. Instead, she lifted her chin, and I knew there was a promise in her gaze. She didn't want another mother to lose her son, and I was right there with her.

"We are strong together. And we will continue to be. But remember, we are Ravenwood, not just a wing. We are Ravenwood. Which means we are with the coven. We are with those who fight against the darkness. My mate is of the coven. And she is now your wing leader, as well. Together, we are stronger."

I looked down at Laurel as she smiled up at me, her eyes filled with tears. "I love you with the deepest part of my soul. My hawk claimed you as mine the moment I saw you when we were children. It took us a while to get here, but now that we are, we are not going back. I will fight to the death for you. And I did. I fought in the In Between for you and will continue to do so. For you, our wing, and our town. I love you, Laurel. I just thought you should know."

Laurel wiped away tears as Sage openly wept in Rome's arms. Others watched us as they began to clap, and Laurel leaned into me and whispered, "Talk about a declaration, hawk boy."

"Whatever you say, fire girl."

"I love you, Jaxton. And you're right. We're stronger together. Now, let's go kick some ass."

"But first, we celebrate. Because if we don't, then what are we fighting for?"

I kissed my mate as the music began again, and people celebrated and mingled, taking our wing one step closer into the future.

The battle would come, and we would be as ready as we could be.

But first, I would be with my mate. And I would never take these moments for granted again.

CHAPTER
TWENTY-TWO

Laurel

"It's time we take the fight to them," Rowen began as we looked around the small pond where Nelle entered the mer realm with the rest of her family and people.

We were here in force, some of our team around the town, but this was where we were doing our best to lure Oriel to us. We had strengthened our protections and done spells over the past week to focus on better centering our magics. We had shined our weapons, sharpened what we could, and protected the hatchlings, cubs, pups, and all those who needed us.

We were ready.

Or as ready as we could be when it came to an unknown force.

"Our trackers can't find Oriel or his hideout. He's using dark magic to hide himself from us, but that means we need to be the ones to take the higher ground when he comes for us. And we will," Rowen said.

"All of us out here will lure the trio in," Jaxton added. I stood by him, my sword in hand, my head raised.

"The fae are taking the perimeter," Aspen informed, and I nodded, knowing that this was important for the fae and the others. The fact that we were trusting the unknown was a big thing. The fae weren't good or bad, it depended on the individual. But their magic was so different than that of the coven and the rest of us. And they kept their secrets. We allowed it because it wasn't our place to say otherwise.

They protected the town just like we did. And we were ready. All of us.

"First, we will do the protection spell," Rowen continued.

"And then we'll add on the luring spell," Sage added with a nod.

I swallowed hard. "And I'm here. Finally."

I saw the small smiles on their faces, as well as on some of the other magical creatures around us. They had all known what was happening to me. There was no hiding it. And they all knew what had happened with

Jaxton, but now here we were, and we were ready—or at least as ready as we could be.

"Let's do this," Sage said, clapping her hands. Rowen and I met each other's gazes. We used to get that excited about doing magic. And then things changed. I had twisted into myself, and Rowen had given too much of herself. But we were finding a way. We had to.

We held hands as the others stood around us, protecting us as well as the town. This was what we had trained for. What we were ready for. We were tired of the revenants coming for us. Now, we would go for them.

I let out a deep breath and began.

"Banish the evil and those who wish harm. Give us courage to pick up our arms. Sisters, brothers, ancestors, friends, our strength is unrivaled and without end. Lords and Ladies, spirit guides, too, guide us and protect us in all we must do. Today is our day, together we rise, victory is ours from earth to skies!"

Warmth soothed my body, and I looked around. Flames danced along my skin, but they didn't hurt. They didn't touch anyone. It was as if it was a part of me. And it was.

I looked behind me as Rowen's eyes widened. A look of surprise shone on her face that shocked me. Rowen never looked nonplussed. She always looked ready to fight anything in front of her. This was different.

I looked over my shoulder, and my eyes widened.

"Okay, then," I whispered. Jaxton came up to me,

sliding his hand over my fiery wing. It didn't burn him. My flame knew its mate, and the hawk in Jaxton's eyes called to me.

"It looks like you'll be flying with me soon, mate of mine."

"That is so cool," Nelle announced as she came forward, blades all down her arms and legs, two in her hands. She was ready to fight, and I knew that Aspen had been teaching her.

I had been doing my best to show her some things, but she was better with a shorter blade than I was.

I saw the consternation in Jaxton's eyes, but he wasn't pulling her back. He would never do that. Instead, he did what he could to protect his sister by making sure she was ready to fight anything that crossed her path.

We would be near the water, as well. So, if she needed to dive in and use her magic there, she could.

We had this.

"Are we ready?" Rowen asked, her voice bellowing.

Everybody nodded, and then Ash joined the circle.

I held my brother's cool hand and swallowed hard.

"Thank you for inviting me," he said dryly, and my lips twitched. Sage just smiled warmly, and Rowen narrowed her eyes.

We needed Ash for this part to lure in the darkness. I hated that we did, but as we had seen before, the darkness was attracted to Ash. Therefore, we would use him. We'd use all of us to get to Oriel so we could take him out.

If we couldn't find him, we would make him find us. And we would be ready.

"Let's do this. Be prepared!" Rowen called out.

"*With perfect love and perfect trust we cast this spell for what we must. Like to like and intentions clear, we conjure the strength to bring darkness near. Our safety paramount, our hearts all pure, we seek the evil that we endure. We call to he who wishes us ill, beckoning thee despite free will. For the good of all, and harm ye none, this is our will, so it will be done!*"

Ash stumbled next to me, and I looked up at Rowen as she nodded quickly. I broke the circle to pick up my brother. Jaxton was on his other side, and Ash pushed us off. "I'm fine. Just caught me by surprise is all."

Whatever it was, we didn't have time to go into it, and I didn't think my brother would let us anyway.

I turned at the first sound of a growl, Rome having shifted to his bear form.

They were here. It had worked.

At least, I hoped it had.

"You called for us?" Renee asked as she fluttered her eyelashes. She had pulled her red curls back from her face, her mate standing next to her. I felt more than saw Jaxton tense next to me at the sight of his cousin. Jaxton's aunt wasn't here, she was back home protecting the hatchlings, and I was glad for that. Because there was no hope for William now, not given what he had done and what we had to do. I wouldn't want his mother to see this.

"What is it you want? To take us down? I don't think so."

"It's time to stop playing around. You say you want this town, but all you do is cause small skirmishes that damage a few buildings. We always rebuild. We always come back." I hadn't meant to say the words since this was supposed to be Rowen's time, but she turned to me and nodded.

So, I kept going.

"Where is your master? You wouldn't be here without his permission. Or would you? Are you like Faith? That stupid where you think you know what you're doing, but you always end up in different situations?"

Renee's eyes narrowed. "You're going to pay for what you did to the sister of my heart."

"And Faith wasn't as strong as my mate," William added, and I had to wonder how stupid the hawk was. He rarely spoke. He was only a good fighter, but Renee had lured him to whatever dark side she was on, and we would have to find a way to change that.

"My revenants are here. You called, and now you have to deal with the ramifications. Just remember, you asked for this. Oh, and Oriel? It's not his time yet. You'll know, honey, when it's time."

"Then I guess it's *your* time, isn't it?" I asked, flames dancing over my sword.

Renee just snorted. "You're so cute. Still not strong enough. But we'll see."

And then she shot out her hands, and fire flew into the middle of the field. My fire pushed it back, as Ash's earth assisted. People moved out of the way, and the fight began.

Revenants slowly crawled out from everywhere, the smoky darkness doing its best to surround us. But Rowen used her air magic to push it back so we weren't cut off from outside forces we may need for help.

The bears and hawks were fighting alongside the coven. Aspen and Nelle were with us, even though the other fae protected the other side of town. The teenage tourist wolves and their mother were with the bears, protecting their young and anyone else they could. We were protecting this town as a unit, many of our forces here doing their best to fight the revenants we'd lured.

And from the sheer numbers, it looked to be hundreds of them. It seemed the spell worked.

Fear spiraled up my spine, but I ignored it and went at Renee. She pulled out a sword of her own, and I rolled my eyes.

"You don't even know how to use that correctly."

"But I know my flame. Battle on, bitch."

Once again, I rolled my eyes at the cliché and went at her. Jaxton flew above me in his hawk form, far bigger than any of the other birds in the air. He went at the revenants, clawing out their eyes and doing his best to take them down as quickly as possible. He was aiming for

William, but Renee's mate did his best to push the revenants towards us.

Ash fought a revenant of his own, watching Rowen's flank so she could use her magic against the smoke that brought in the revenants. I stabbed my sword into the closest revenant, then went at Renee again. Our swords clanged, fire dancing around us. Suddenly, Sage was there, Rome at her side as she used her water magic to douse any flames that got too close to the forest or anyone else.

We had practiced this. We could do this. But Renee was mine.

It was sword against sword, fire against fire as the others fought around us. Rome tackled another revenant, ripping off its head before going for another. Finally, William and Jaxton got closer, claws and talons in the air as they fought one another. But I couldn't focus on them. I had to focus on Renee.

"Your mate is going to die. My mate is much stronger."

"You're delusional. Why are you fighting for a man we don't even know? Does Oriel even exist?"

"Of course, my master exists. He's the one who will win this town and its magic. And that little air bitch over there." She shot her finger in Rowen's direction. "You really think you're strong enough for this? You never were. You might have come back as a phoenix, but you don't even know how to tap into that power. You would be so much stronger as a necromancer."

"I will never fight for your side."

"Then you're not going to fight at all. But first, there's something my master asked of me."

She pulled out a dagger, set it aflame, and threw it into the air.

I reached out with my flame, trying to stop it, but I couldn't. Instead, Renee's sword slammed into my side, cutting through the flesh and searing it as I screamed, falling to my knees. Jaxton turned to me, pushing William off him. And then I couldn't breathe. Not through the pain. Not through the shock.

Almost as soon as I hit the ground, Nelle let out a shocked gasp and looked down at the fiery dagger in her heart, then she fell, too.

There was a scream, another shout. And it felt as if the world had ended.

The beautiful goth mermaid with her kohl-rimmed eyes, her chainmail leathers, and her dark, flowing hair lay on the ground, blood pooling around her as the fae king screamed, and the hawk wing leader swooped in.

I couldn't breathe.

TWENTY-THREE

Jaxton

My talons slashed into William. This couldn't be happening. I could not believe this was happening. I should have left her with her father. I should have hidden her back in the water with the other mermaids. They would have been able to protect her. Instead... Dear God. Not now.

The ground shook, the air pulsed, and I looked down to see Aspen kneeling over Nelle, his entire body shaking as he grieved. He screamed, and trees uprooted, other revenants dissolved and burst into a thousand pieces.

The shifters were unhurt, as was the coven. Even in grief, the fae king didn't harm his allies. No, Aspen was using too much power too quickly in his misery and hurting those who had hurt his mate.

Because that's who Nelle was to him. His mate.

And now she was gone. I had lost my sister.

I flew closer, trying to get through whatever magic was coming forward, attempting to get to my sibling.

Instead, she stared up at me with lifeless gray eyes, her mouth parted, blood pooling around her. A small trickle of blood trickled out of her mouth, and then I screamed.

A collective of shrieks echoed back at me, my hawks grieving with me.

She was ours. She was mine. And now, she was gone.

I looked down at Laurel as she fought Renee, my mate bleeding from her side from a wound that had been licked with fire. Renee had cut her, injured her, but Laurel was giving back just as strong. Slash slash slash. Clang clang clang.

Sword against sword, fire against fire, the two were equally matched. Only my phoenix needed to catch the dark witch in order to dig into her new powers and fight back. I didn't know if we knew how. I needed to get to Nelle, to my baby sister, but first, I needed to make Renee hurt.

I whirled in the air, my talons outstretched as I clawed at William. My cousin was my size, maybe slightly smaller in the wingspan, but whatever magic pounded through him thanks to Renee's darkness, made him stronger.

Somehow, he was stronger than me. But he would not win this. I refused to let this traitor, this asshole who mated my sister's killer, get the upper hand.

William flipped around me and latched his talons to my chest. I did the same with him, and we whirled in the air, spiraling down to the ground. Others scattered for me, and I saw Rome try to move to catch us, but I shouted at him with a screech to not come closer.

The bear seemed to understand and went to guard his mate, fighting alongside the new witch with all of their combined strength.

William and I unlatched from each other at the last instant before hitting the ground and shifting to human.

It didn't matter that we were naked. Shifters didn't care. I needed to stop William.

"That stupid bitch of a sister of yours didn't deserve to live. She wasn't even a pureblood. She shifted into a fish. We eat fish. Don't you understand that? Your mother was a traitor for opening her legs to the mermaid king. And now your sister's where she should be."

Vengeance coursed through me. I needed to stop this. I needed to end this man. I needed to destroy everything he held dear before I turned to the darkness that threatened us all.

"What happened to you?" I needed to know. I needed

to know where my sweet cousin had gone and why this man was here in his place, a traitor to us all.

"You treated me like I was nothing. Now, you deserve what you get. Nelle is gone. And soon, we'll kill your bitch of a mate. And then we're going after the wing. I will be the wing leader. What I should've always been."

"You've always been delusional."

"No more than you."

We shifted back to hawk form, our talons outstretched. William went for my eyes, and I twisted, earning a claw in the ribs instead. I snapped and clawed at him, both of us fighting for our lives.

We weren't like bears or wolves that could fight on the ground. We needed to be up in the air, but our talons were deadly. The strength of our beaks enough to break bone. We could kill, maim, torture.

But I wanted William gone fast. I wanted vengeance.

I wanted my little sister back.

William twisted, going after Laurel this time, angling his wings to shoot like a bullet. And that was it. I couldn't let him live.

I moved down, angling myself, and raked my talons down his back. I twisted in the air and slammed him into the ground as we both tumbled and shifted back to human. Blood coated our bodies, and still I went after him, my fingers shifting to talons as I clawed and swiped. William did the same, catching me in my shoulder. I got his hip. He punched me in the face, and I kneed him in the gut.

I looked at him then, saw how Renee kept fighting Laurel, flames dancing all around us. Magic pulsed through me, and I pulled on the strength of the wing. I felt their hope, their fear, their passion as shifters.

Aiden, my mother, everyone. They were all a part of me. William wasn't. Our bonds had been broken. He was lost to us forever.

I looked at my cousin and knew he saw the moment I had gained in power. The moment I became the true wing leader. I dug my talons into his chest, gripping his heart. Then, I twisted it.

The light in his eyes dimmed, and for a moment, I saw the young boy who had once trailed after us. The one who had once been my friend. But then, he was gone.

Only a traitor remained, the darkness seeping into his eyes as his mate called out for him.

My cousin was dead, his blood on my hands, but the battle wasn't over.

"No! How dare you?" Renee screamed. I shifted back, going after Renee and helping Laurel. But Laurel seemed to have the upper hand, even before more magic filled the field. Something unknown that I had never felt before.

I turned, shifting back to human and knowing I would exhaust myself if I weren't careful. Aiden tossed me a pair of sweats that I pulled on quickly and gripped a sword that had fallen in battle. I cut off a revenant's head and moved towards Aspen, wondering what the hell was going on.

The fae king looked at me, his eyes glowing green swirls. "She was sacrificed with a spell of fire, it's not true death. That spell was meant only for her. That blade dipped in a poison just for her. That means she's mine now."

I frowned, confused as everyone continued fighting around us. I needed to get back to Laurel, and yet as Aspen stood there, holding my sister in his arms, I had to wonder what the hell the fae was doing. What had he meant?

"What's going on?" I called out over the shouts.

"The dagger was spell-soaked. It's not a true death. I can bring her back."

Alarm flooded me, and I swallowed hard. "Not as a revenant. Not if she's a shade."

"No, I can still feel the bonds. She's like you were, caught in the In Between. I can bring her back."

Aspen's gaze narrowed, even as his body glowed. "What will that do to her?" I asked, hope and a kernel of joy in me mixing with the fear.

"She'll be mine. Forever. She will be a mermaid, still a hawk, but she will also be the fae queen. She will be mine."

Did I have the right to allow him to make that choice for her? Then again, I didn't think I could stop Aspen.

So, instead, I leaned forward, kissed my sister on the

forehead, and met the fae king's eyes. "Save her. I need to help my mate."

"It is done."

Magic so old it tasted of the beginnings of time coated my tongue and my body and everywhere else. Everybody froze as they turned as one towards the fae king, my sister in his arms.

The pair lit up like a beacon, magic I didn't understand coming towards us. Even Rowen looked surprised, her mouth parting as she held onto the magic that kept the shadows at bay, Ash at her side, protecting her.

"She is mine," Aspen repeated. The magic pulsed again, and again and again, faster and faster until my heartbeat raced with it.

Nelle arched in Aspen's hold, her body convulsing for a moment as a shout echoed. I wanted to stop this, I needed to ease her pain, but I didn't know what exactly was happening.

Suddenly, sea-foam green tattoos appeared all over her arms, her chest, and her hips, matching those on Aspen, and I knew that he had created a mating bond to protect her.

That was the spell.

His mate was alive, just like mine fought behind me.

Aspen met my gaze and nodded. "I will protect her." And then they were gone, leaving a trail of sea-foam green glitter where they had both been standing. I had to wonder what the hell I had just seen.

As if someone had popped a balloon in a vacuum, the fighting continued as if none of that had happened at all. Maybe I was just losing my mind. I turned towards Laurel, saw her battling Renee, and knew that I needed to protect her. My mate. My future.

And damn anyone who got in my way.

CHAPTER
TWENTY-FOUR

Laurel

T honestly couldn't believe what I was seeing, but I couldn't focus on the others. I needed to focus on the bitch in front of me. Renee screamed, grief pouring off her in waves, and yet I couldn't feel sorry for her. She had used her mate and his connections. It was clear that while she might have loved him in her own way, their darkness had twisted each of them, and I didn't know what any of that meant. I didn't know if she *could* actually love him. Not the way she should. Not in a way that mattered.

I could barely even breathe through the pain of possibly losing my mate again, and yet she had *used* William. And she was trying to kill those I loved. Again and again and again.

I shouted, doing my best to breathe and focus on the magic within me. My wings pulsated, ripping from my back as flame arched over me.

Renee tossed her sword down, and I did the same, only magic between us. The swords got in our way, at least when it came to her.

"You're going to pay for that!" she screamed as she tossed fire towards Jaxton as he ran towards me. I threw myself in front of her, not realizing that my feet were off the ground. I was *flying* towards her. I staggered in the air for a bit, unused to these wings of mine. When Jaxton shifted into a hawk, flying at my side, I knew this was what I needed to do. I let the fire within me take control. Finally, I just let go.

I had been holding back with the curse, keeping the power within me tethered for so long. Now, I could push. I moved my hands forward, palms outstretched as fire slid through my pores and out towards Renee. She opened her mouth and screamed, throwing fire at me once again.

Somehow, she was still maintaining her power over the revenants. Suddenly, I knew it wasn't just her this time. Oriel must be near, or at least watching or doing something, because this was not only her necromancer power. This was something else. Some*one* else. Someone far stronger, much darker. He was using his power alongside Renee's, even if he wasn't standing in the field with us. He was somewhere. I knew it. Maybe we were a distraction. But I didn't know. All I knew was that I needed to take out Renee. I needed to stop her before she hurt anyone else I loved.

I couldn't focus on the fact that Nelle might be gone. I couldn't think about anything but trying to get Renee. The witch planted both feet in the ground as I moved towards her, and then she screamed, pouring a wave of fire at me. My wings fluttered, and I stopped the flames before they came, shouting. When I lowered to the ground, my wings aching, I looked at my friends, at my coven, and saw all their eyes wide.

"That's a fucking beautiful sight." Rome grinned as he came to my side as they fought off each revenant.

Renee had positioned herself behind the line of undead, and we had to get closer.

The town wouldn't be able to survive the onslaught for long. I didn't even know what was happening on the other parts of the border. All I knew was that we needed to protect those we loved.

We needed to keep the revenants here where we could handle them. That way, no one else got hurt because of our mistakes. No longer.

"One more spell. Do you have it in you?" Rowen called, and I grinned wildly, my wings beating behind me.

"Hell, yeah, I do."

And then the sister of my heart smiled, and I knew she saw the power within me, even as the battle raged around us. Because I was no longer the cursed one. I was strength. I was fire. I was witch. I was coven. And we could do this.

Jaxton held one of my hands, Ash the other as Rowen stood next to him and then Rome and then Sage approached. We were the six. We were of the coven, yet we were more. We were everything that we needed to be, and we would banish this woman.

"Repeat after me," Rowen began, and I did so.

"*Our might is right and spirits rise, strength of six across the skies. Take this evil, make them pay. Give us strength to win the day. The darkest reign this day will end, giving us time to gather and mend. This sacred truth we do decree, this is our will, so mote it be!*"

Power surged within me, my wings beating a mile a minute, and then we were off, the revenants falling to the ground as they were pushed away with our magic. The smoke billowed, the darkness no longer encroaching. We could fight now, and we could win.

I just needed to get to Renee.

My sword was no longer there, Renee having burned it to ash, but that was fine. I could still get closer. I could still fight.

I ran, my wings beating as I tried to lift off and couldn't, and then Rowen pushed out air magic, and Ash used his earth while Rome pounded his paws into the ground next to me, and Sage used her water power. They pushed me forward and up, increasing my magic and my strength, my connection to Mother Earth and everything around me.

This was what we had been practicing, what we needed. This was what the coven was for. This was why we *could* save Ravenwood.

I had never had so much hope before, and I knew this was it. I knew this was how we could make it.

And then Jaxton was there in hawk form, flying around me, using his wings to teach me how to soar. And then I was off. I shot off into the air, and Sage let out a whoop before going back to fighting her own battles.

Jaxton and I went after Renee. The dark witch threw a blade of flame, but I stopped it before it got to my mate, angry that she would even dare try to hurt what was mine.

I looked at Jaxton in the air, his hawk form tilting a bit to give me a slight wave, and then we were off once again. He slashed at Renee with his talons, and I used my flame. It was battle against battle, heat against heat.

Renee was strong, but finally, *finally*, I was stronger.

I no longer felt as if I were being burned from the inside out just trying to breathe.

I scorched the earth purposefully now, pushing at what I could. I knew this could be the end. This could be it.

"You will never have this town," I called as the others cheered behind me. "Ravenwood is ours."

"It was never yours. You are on stolen land. This was ours, and you will finally know it."

Renee slid both hands into the air, lightning shooting down into the ground around us. Lightning so much like the storm that had brought Sage to us.

And then a wolf in the darkness blinked at us, his eyes red. Suddenly, he was gone, and I couldn't think. Was that Oriel? Or something else?

Renee pushed fire at me again, and I did the same, our two plumes slamming into one another, arcing into a wave that took the rest of the coven's power to keep confined so it didn't burn down the town I was trying to save.

"Keep her focused. We'll get her," Rowen called out over the din of the roaring flames. I nodded, doing my part. I needed to keep Renee focused on me so the others could come at her.

I slashed out with blade after blade of fire as talons ripped into Renee's side, trying to get through her personal wards. Renee fell to the ground, burns scorching her, blood pooling, and looked at me with wide eyes. I knew this could be the end. We were almost there—one step closer to Oriel and protecting our town.

And then a shockwave ran through us, and I flew back, hitting my head on the ground. Jaxton let out a pained sound as he landed next to me, and I went to him, both of us in human form now, holding onto one another as the ground shook and an earthquake carved a jagged line through the earth. I looked around to make sure we were all safe. Everybody was alive, but something was coming. Something was happening. Was this Oriel? Finally?

Smoke twisted around like a chain over Renee's body. She gave me a wicked grin and glare, and then she was gone. The smoke had taken her, taken our enemy. It seemed the battle was over. For now.

I looked at my mate, then the others, then back at Jaxton before crushing my mouth to his, praying that we could rest if only for a moment.

We might have lost Renee, but we would find her again. I had to hope.

And then Ash's hand was on my shoulder, pulling me up, and my brother held me.

I sank against my mate after Ash let me go and looked around at the members of the town who had come together to protect it, and I had to hope that we would be enough.

I had to have faith that we would find the strength to save Ravenwood. Once and for all.

CHAPTER
TWENTY-FIVE

Oriel

Oriel set Renee down on the bed and whispered words of healing under his breath. The burns and scrapes began to close, even though they wouldn't fully fade away. She would carry scars, but then again, she probably deserved them. She had failed. They all had failed. And now, he would have to get his hands dirty.

Oriel sighed and patted Renee's broken cheek. "You did your best. But we are not finished yet."

"He killed my mate," she sputtered, her voice raw from screaming.

"William was weak. But you knew that."

"He was mine," she snapped.

"And he is no longer. I do regret his loss, just as I regret Faith's. But needs are met, and now we have access to the core."

She narrowed her eyes. "You used me as a distraction."

Oriel grinned. "Of course, I did." He let out a sigh. "What did you think I would do? Watch you make mistake after mistake? No, you did what you were supposed to do, just like William, just like Faith. But now I have access to the core of Ravenwood, and it will be ours."

Mine.

Oriel sneered. It would be his alone, but he didn't say that.

"Then what's next?" she asked, pressing her hand to her wound.

"We heal you, we gather our forces, and then we finally take the town and the coven. And I take what's mine."

Renee passed out in pain, a small smile playing on her lips. She may grieve her mate, but she would mourn the power lost more if they weren't careful.

Oriel shook his head and then turned on his heel, making his way to look out the window. He saw the town of Ravenwood below, although Rowen and anyone else would never know he was here. That was the strength of his magic. They would never know he had access to the power that was Ravenwood. Or that it was *his.*

He smiled and tapped his fingers to the glass, waiting for the right time.

"Okay, dear sister. You might have killed some of my team, but it was all written. Now, you'll have to deal with me. You thought you were the last of the Ravenwoods? Oh, no, dear sister, how wrong you were. And soon, you'll realize exactly how wrong you have always been. And how wrong you will always be."

CHAPTER
TWENTY-SIX

Jaxton

My phoenix rode me, her grin fierce as she arched her hips, her pussy clamped like a vise around my cock. I reached up, brushed my thumbs across her nipples as she lowered her head, her fiery curls dancing around us. Her hair had gotten even redder after she came back and every time she turned into a phoenix, as if she were turning into pure flame, heart, and fire. And she was all mine.

I grinned and lifted my hips as I pounded into her. She rolled her hips above me, meeting me thrust for thrust.

"Fuck me harder, hawk of mine."

"As long as you fuck me right back, witch." She

grinned and leaned down to kiss me before I turned us both, putting her on her hands and knees. I gripped her hips, her fiery wings flowing out around us, and grinned as I fucked her. I pounded into her as she arched back for me, flames dancing around us. My hawk flew around the mating bond to meet her anchor.

I had never known sex could be like this, that this kind of power could infiltrate us both, but this was everything.

When she came, she rolled her body back, her back to my chest, and I slid my fingers over her clit, my hands on her breasts as I bit down on her neck, claiming her as mine. She moaned my name, and then I filled her, coming hard as both of us shook. We fell to the bed, her wings disappearing into smoke as we kissed, loved, and simply lay there.

She looked up at me afterward as both of us lazily drew imaginary pictures over our anchors.

"Is it getting hotter, or is it just me?"

"Is that a line?" I asked with a laugh.

"I can't believe this is our future," she whispered.

"I can't believe I almost lost you again."

I would never forget the look on Renee's face as she tried to kill Laurel, again and again, or the fact that we had only lost that part of the battle because of Oriel. A man we hadn't seen, but we knew the taste of his power.

I leaned down and brushed my lips across hers, then nuzzled her and peppered more kisses down her neck and her chest as I sucked on her breasts. I couldn't help it. I needed her taste on my tongue. My hand was still between her legs, gently playing with her slick folds, just us waking up in the morning before we had to meet with the coven to plan.

"Tomorrow, we will fight again, and again after, but we are stronger now than ever."

I nodded, kissed her again, and removed my hand so I could hug her, hold her.

"And your sister's safe?"

I cringed. "Let's not talk about my sister while we're naked and spooning."

"Well, is she?"

I nodded, knowing it was important that we spoke of the details, even if it didn't feel like this was the time. "Nelle will be within the fae lands for a while as she heals, but then she'll be back." I paused. "Her father is coming to visit."

Laurel almost shot up off the bed. "The king of the mermaids is coming here to Ravenwood?"

"It seems like. There's more than just Ravenwood now against Oriel. And the merpeople are spread out all over the world." My mother had been working with her mate to speak to the others of the world to see what could be done. Ravenwood was important to the world for many reasons, and not just because it was the home of *my* heart.

We both took a minute to focus on that before I held her close and kissed her again.

"Okay, then. Things are happening."

I nodded. "Quicker than any of us thought."

Soon, we'd meet with the coven to make more plans for Oriel and for Ravenwood itself. For now, my sister was safe, stronger than ever—possibly even stronger than me.

My mate was whole, a power in her own right.

And we all had a purpose. The wing was strong. Coming into the future and navigating their own mistakes while rising above them.

We had plans. A future.

It had almost taken losing everything more than once for that to happen, but it *was* happening.

We were beyond dawn, beyond the dusk, turning into the next phase of our prophecy and path.

In the end, as I held my mate, I knew that we would have to get up soon, but I ignored all of it. I kissed Laurel, wondering how I was so lucky to finally be able to hold the woman I loved, the woman I had lost. The woman that was mine until the end of time.

TWENTY-SEVEN

Rowen

I was used to being alone. I had been alone for most of my life. My parents were gone. My family was gone. I was the last of the Ravenwoods. Named after an ancestor, and yet alone. It had taken years for our coven to become what it was. To find out who we could be if curses were broken, and we could find who we needed to be. And yet, I had almost lost all of that—multiple times.

Sage was back. No longer a distant memory of what I missed and what we had all forgotten. She was no longer being pushed away from the town because of a curse.

I moved into the kitchen, pulled out a bottle of pinot

noir, uncorked it, and slowly poured myself a full glass. I considered drinking straight from the bottle after the events of that day, but I knew as I took a deep sip of my wine, the smoky flavor settling on my tongue, that I needed to sit in my meditation room and focus. I needed to set up my crystals and replenish the power that I had lost in that battle. Battle after battle, year after year, it wasn't enough. I wasn't enough.

But that was why we had a coven. That was why we had a prophecy set in stone for how we would fight the darkness. And that darkness was Oriel. It had always been, and yet he was strong enough to get past me. He'd hidden from me for so long that I hadn't known exactly who was coming, and I still didn't. Not until he was right in my face. That was because I wasn't strong enough. I had never been. And that wasn't like me. I needed to be strong enough. But then again, maybe that wasn't the case. Maybe it couldn't be the case.

Sage hadn't been pushed away because of a spell of the town's making. It had been Oriel. That was the only explanation. The town wouldn't have pushed away one of its founding members. We wouldn't have forgotten that she existed at times, or not known to pull her in until it was almost too late. That had to be Oriel. This necromancer was a power that I didn't understand, and I hated that I didn't. I needed to understand, and yet it wasn't enough. How was I yet again not enough?

And then there was Laurel. Laurel, the sister of my

heart and my coven member, the one who I had never been able to find a way to protect. I had put my heart and soul into finding new spells and ways to rip that curse from her. Only every time I did, it only hurt her worse, and I could feel it. Along our coven bonds, I felt the flames burning her, and there was nothing I could do. I would scream in my dreams as she burned and faded, and there was nothing I could do because of the Christopher curse. Because of something from long ago before we were born.

I took another sip of my drink and looked around my ancestral home that was far too big for one person.

I didn't even have a familiar. I had lost my cat Samuel three years ago to old age. I hadn't wanted to lengthen his life using a spell, coming so close to dark magic and necromancy that it would twist my soul. So, I had said goodbye to him, to my heart, much like I had said goodbye to everyone else.

We had lost Trace, Penelope, Alden, William. We had lost countless others in the fights against Oriel and those he sent after us. I had nearly lost the family of my making, Nelle, and so many others.

And every time I tried to formulate a plan to go at Oriel head-to-head, he wouldn't let us. He was the one in control. I was the Ravenwood witch. I was a formidable power. And yet, I could not win in this.

I'd lost.

And I didn't even know how.

I felt him near the wards of my home even before he hit my doorstep.

I had known he would come.

I would always know when he was there, even if I told myself that he shouldn't be. That I wasn't that woman.

I opened the door, wine in hand, and looked at Ash.

He was the boy I'd loved. But I didn't recognize the man.

He stood there in his thousand-dollar suit, shirt unbuttoned at the top, his hair falling over his face. He was gorgeous, seemingly sculpted from stone with a jawline made of granite. His dark, piercing eyes were far darker than they had ever been before.

He was of the Christopher line, Laurel's brother, but he was also the man of my heart, the man of my past. But not of my future.

"I know we planned with the group, but it's our turn, Rowen. It's time for us to come together so we can fight the darkness."

He said the words, but there was nothing in them. No emotion, no feeling. Nothing.

It was as if he said the words by rote, and I couldn't recognize the man that stood in front of me.

I sipped my drink and took a step back. "Come in, Ash. I suppose it's time we talked."

He walked past me, gently brushing his arm against mine, and I knew it was an accident. He wouldn't even do it instinctually. He didn't have the capacity any longer.

I closed the door, swallowed my emotions. Because he wasn't mine anymore—maybe he had never been.

I pressed my palm to the aged wood of my door, ensured the town's wards that were slowly draining me dry despite the coven's help were intact, as well as the wards around my home, and then closed it. When I turned to my soulmate, I met his gaze.

Could a person be a soulmate to someone without a soul?

That was the question for the ages. The question of my past and my future.

Ash Christopher was my soulmate. My path.

But he had lost his soul.

And he could never be mine.

Ash and Rowen's romance completes the Ravenwood Coven Trilogy in Evernight Unleashed.
Finally.

A Note from Carrie Ann Ryan

Thank you so much for reading **DUSK UNVEILED!**

I love writing paranormal romance and a few friends of mine have been betting the universe for witches, covens, and girl power books and that is what sparked the idea of the town of Ravenwood. I cannot wait to show you more of this world!

Next in the series is Evernight Unleashed. And you guys...I can't even begin to tell you what Ash and Rowen are about to go through...and yet...they are so much stronger than the world thinks they are. Just you wait!

The Ravenwood Coven Series:
Book 1: Dawn Unearthed
Book 2: Dusk Unveiled
Book 3: Evernight Unleashed

While you wait for more witches, try the Talon Pack series!

The Talon Pack:

Book 1: Tattered Loyalties

Book 2: An Alpha's Choice

Book 3: Mated in Mist

Book 4: Wolf Betrayed

Book 5: Fractured Silence

Book 6: Destiny Disgraced

Book 7: Eternal Mourning

Book 8: Strength Enduring

Book 9: Forever Broken

Book 10: Mated in Darkness

The Aspen Pack Series:

Book 1: Etched in Honor

If you want to make sure you know what's coming next from me, you can sign up for my newsletter at www. CarrieAnnRyan.com; follow me on twitter at @CarrieAnnRyan, or like my Facebook page. I also have a Facebook Fan Club where we have trivia, chats, and other goodies. You guys are the reason I get to do what I do and I thank you.

Make sure you're signed up for my MAILING LIST so you can know when the next releases are available as well as find giveaways and FREE READS.

Happy Reading!

Want to keep up to date with the next Carrie Ann Ryan Release? Receive Text Alerts easily!

Text CARRIE to 210-741-8720

ABOUT THE AUTHOR

Carrie Ann Ryan is the New York Times and USA Today bestselling author of contemporary, paranormal, and young adult romance. Her works include the Montgomery Ink, Redwood Pack, Fractured Connections, and Elements of Five series, which have sold over 3.0 million books worldwide. She started writing while in graduate school for her advanced degree in chemistry and hasn't stopped since. Carrie Ann has written over seventy-five novels and novellas with more in the works. When she's not losing herself in her emotional and action-packed worlds, she's reading as much as she can while wrangling her clowder of cats who have more followers than she does.

www.CarrieAnnRyan.com